To Let a Tiger Be

To Let a Tiger Be

Trevor Farrell

Second Printing: 2019

ISBN: 978-0-359-72428-4

This is a work of fiction. Names, characters, businesses, places, events, locales, and incidents are either the products of the author's imagination or used in a fictitious manner. Any resemblance to actual persons, living or dead, or actual events is purely coincidental.

Mathemagician Paperbacks

mathemagician@trevorfarrell.com

www.trevorfarrell.com

This novel is dedicated to Nicholas.

Take that, you evil bastard.

Preface

Just what the heck are you reading the preface for?

I honestly never could understand the practice of jam-packing a book with acknowledgements, dedications, forwards, a preface, author's notes, introductions, etc. etc. I've found that in my own personal experience, you can tell an awful lot about a book – be it genre fiction or fine literature – by just how much of what the author decides to slip in between the covers that *isn't* the meat of the final product. This is particularly so in the case of "classic" works of literature that have aged exceptionally poorly: I come across works where various glossaries, appendices, footnotes, etc., outweigh the meat of the story itself.

Unless it's absolutely justified, I just can't stand it. I firmly believe that the narrative should speak for itself, and that the reader shouldn't be patronized with explanations at every turn. Part of the joy in reading a story, after all, lies in analyzing and understanding the premise. It's an act of critical thinking: the joke isn't ever as funny if somebody's explaining every part of it to you along the way.

Now, if you're one of *those* strange people who's still reading a silly, rambling preface by *this* point – perhaps out of the meager hope for more gleefully recalcitrant remarks – then I might as well get on with it and describe the thought process that led to *To Let a Tiger Be*.

The vague outlines of the idea had been brewing in my head for quite some time, but what ultimately got the whole thing started was a simple writing prompt, framed in the form of a Quora question: 'Can you write a sad story with a twist happy ending?' I forced myself to start writing an entry, and as so often happens during the creative process, it all seemed like it was over too quickly. A short story – unbeknownst to me to be chapter one – sitting before me, published to Quora, on September 25th, 2018.

Much to my surprise and dismay, the short story received almost no attention whatsoever.

I was dissatisfied, of course, but the experience came with an invaluable lesson – the important thing about the story, after all, was that *I* found something of value in it. I was proud of it. And I wasn't going to let it die so quickly.

And so, I kept writing.

I wrote another short story, of similar theme, but with a little more exposition, and with slightly different characters. It gained a little more traction with my followers, family and friends.

And so, I kept writing.

I wrote another short story, with different characters – some of which knew the characters from previous chapters – and in a slightly varied setting.

I can't say it was easy. That's really not the right word for it at all. Perhaps 'confusing' is a better word. But nonetheless, somewhere along the lines, I looked back and found myself about thirty thousand words deep into a science fiction story. Standing there, completely unprepared, I decided that I'd call it a first draft.

To Let a Tiger Be is my first novel and is thus something that I hold with a sort of pessimistic pride: I acknowledge that it's most certainly riddled with errors. Like many of my works, I'm sure I'll look back on this with a sense of embarrassment over all the little mistakes that I didn't know I was making at the time. But the fact of the matter is that I can't ever hope to write my 50th novel until I've finished up my first.

I am convinced that there isn't a single decent work of science fiction out there that *isn't* a subtle commentary on real world issues, ranging from social to political; *To Let a Tiger Be* is no exception. So, I sat down and thought about the issues that meant the most to me. Issues that I thought I might have had something important to say about.

This is a story about discrimination. It doesn't matter what kind, mind you – they all work off the same basic principles of hating and distancing ourselves from what we find alien, based off trivial differences. The question that I present, dear reader, is this: as time goes on, humanity has generally found itself growing more tolerant, peaceful, and accepting. But what will happen when this mindset it brought to its logical extreme? How will humanity react when we are faced with something so strange, so dissimilar to our own, that it pushes our ability to tolerate and accept towards its breaking point? Would we learn how to accept one another, as we've proven ourselves to be generally decent at doing? Or are we as a collective, deep down inside, no different than any other hateful animal?

There are other themes that this story tackles – ideas about a world of mass production, largely uninvolving a human workforce. Ideas about what it means to be a human, what it means to be a person, and what it means to be alive. Ideas about time and change and mechanical cats. But none of those ideas were as important to me as *that* idea.

-    Trevor Farrell

Chapter 1

Project Log Day 3,376

"I hereby pronounce you husband and wife."

Their lips touched and the crowd burst into roaring applause. Although she had registered it upon entering the chapel, it was only now that, for whatever reason, that Katie considered the louder cheering coming from one side of the nave than the other. In fact, aside from a few colleagues and professors from her university – Brian, Becky, Sarah, Jennifer – it was almost entirely Robert's family that dared to attend. And as much as her heart was racing, it sunk a little in her chest at the realization.

She hated her mind for it. Out of all of the possible moments that it could bother to turn on her insecurities, it had to now. She ought to be happy.

As they walked down the center of the nave, they paused together before the large oak doors of the chapel. She could feel the slight tremor in his grip, and as she looked up at his expression, she noticed how hard he was working to hide his apprehensions.

Finally, he took a deep breath and turned to her, a glimmer of hope dancing across his face in the form of a faint smile. "Ready?" It was just a little too enthusiastic to be genuine.

"Yes," she lied. But it was okay. They both knew it, and they both felt the same way. Somehow, that made it better.

The doors opened, and the morning sunlight flooded in. The crowd was larger than she could have ever reasonably expected. Her eyes darted across the picket signs. From face to ugly, angry, hating face. She tried her best to block out the slurs she saw and heard, but it didn't take long to overwhelm her. The worry found its grip: could she be certain that the police force was adequate to hold back the mob? Were their escorts enough?

Robert held her a little closer, and it made her feel a little better about everything. As they walked down the steps, a woman leapt over the temporary metal fence and came towards Robert.

"You sick son of a fucking whore!"

Two officers jumped in and stopped the woman, each making quick work of holding her to the ground. In response to the excitement, the crowd got louder. Somewhere, a loudspeaker blared unintelligible commands at the unwelcome audience. Katie didn't even realize how tightly she was clutching Robert until she realized he was holding her every bit as tightly. The bodyguards next to them spoke something that was lost to the noise and motioned to the line of cars. Robert and Katie made haste towards the nearest open door and stepped inside. It was closed behind them, and everything became quiet again, as the automated vehicle carried them away.

The sun was only a soft orange glow that lay hidden just behind the horizon by the time the small mechanical hummingbird made its routine visit to the electric tree. As it hovered, its head turned to scan the abandoned house. Then, back again to scan up and down the silver trunk and the blue shimmery leaves – a combination carbon sink and energy generator, and certainly a machine of aesthetic significance. One of many produced and distributed en masse, now laid to rest in an overwrought backyard.

The hummingbird fluttered up to the nearest flower in its branches and plugged its beak into the appropriate port in its array. Its LED eyes went from a dull glow to a bright, rapid flashing. Once all the energy from the flower's capacitor was drained, it flew off to the next one, repeating the process until the cells in its belly were full. Content at last, or at least for the night, it flew off into the night sky in search for a resting spot.

The suburbs of San Diego County were once considered a baseline standard of attainability for those who appreciated spacious living and a large front yard to themselves. Naturally, they were the first to go after the crash. Since the exodus, nature had come to reclaim what was rightfully hers. Cracks in the roads and sidewalks made way for tall grass. Ivy had overgrown the once-proud homes.

The little mechanical hummingbird found its small, secluded branch in its favorite tree and came to rest. It folded its wings in, lifted its head, and dimmed its eyes to a close. With its hibernation initiated, it set an internal alarm clock to awaken it bright and early the next morning.

It was at this exact moment that a mechanical cat, who had been crouched and waiting patiently with cold motors since the late afternoon, pounced upon the sleeping hummingbird, knocking its body from the tree. Disoriented and confused, the little electric creature attempted to take off, but found itself trapped under the metallic paw of the imitation feline. Eyes glowing orange, the cat lowered its maw upon the bird and pressed down. The hummingbird went limp, its eyes void, and the cat's eyes pulsated once. It released its limp body and batted at it a few times. Satisfied with its demise, the cat plucked it up in its mouth and trotting back to its home across the street. Hummingbirds didn't ever provide her with very much energy, not nearly enough to satiate herself, but that wasn't its only purpose.

The cat clamored up the stairs and entered her loft in the corner of the room. Stepping around a small pile of parts – components that once used to make squirrels, mice, and birds. She dropped the hummingbird in its designated spot and scanned her inventory of components with impeccable concentration one last time, ensuring that no individual part was missing. Satisfied at last, she got to work.

With only the efforts of her own mouth and paws, combined with limited influence of her radio transmissions upon each of the designated receivers, she began the long process of meticulously reassembling the parts. A nudge here, a careful push here. Commanding the pieces together into a form of her choosing. In was a tiring process, but not a fruitless one.

With her final product before her, she gingerly plucked it up by its scruff and carried it over to the stack of blankets she called her bed.

Setting it down carefully, she concentrated, the energy flowing from her teeth. When enough was enough, she let go and stood back to survey the results.

The kitten's eyes opened with a soft orange glow as it looked up towards its mother. With its company acknowledged, it let out a meek electronic mew. It was already rather large, much more than a biological kitten would need to be at birth, and the electrical requirement for its creation had taken a toll on the mother. She gently placed her chin on her child's forehead and emitted a signal of reassurance. Comfort. Stay put for mommy. Once the mewing had subsided, she got up and trotted away, wasting no time in her search for the energy needed to feed her child.

The sun had set by the time that the motorcade had split away from Robert and Katie's automated vehicle. At this point in the journey, it was unlikely that anybody was following them – even the fastest of drones would have petered out by now. All that remained was the quiet hum of the electric motor and the tone the wheels made as they coasted across the pavement. Katie let herself relax a little bit, now that everything was behind them again.

With her mind at ease, curiosity finally got the better of her. Just what sort of a scene were they leaving behind? Was everybody alright? Had the crowd dispersed? She turned on the network and started surveying the reaction.

Robert took notice and sighed, his shoulders drooping. "Oh Katie... you promised you wouldn't do that."

Katie blushed and lowered her head. "I know, I'm sorry. It's just..." she sighed and closed her eyes. "It's been a lot to think about. It's hard to ignore, and I need some closure. That's all."

He thought for a moment. "Well, if you really can't help yourself, at least let me be a part of it. We're together in this now, and there's no turning back from that. Why don't you put on what you're watching for me to watch with you?"

Katie turned off her personal receiver and turned on the screen embedded in the dashboard. The flickering light portrayed an interview in progress between a portly, greying man and an interviewer with darker skin and a sharp business dress.

"...Now then, Mr. Hegarty, I'd like to point to the statistics of the matter. The data suggests that over eighty percent of American citizens are proponents of the bill's passage. As somebody who disagrees with the popular opinion, what do you think this says about the United States as a whole?"

"Well, Mrs. Warren, I'd call it a surefire sign of our failure as a nation. That someth-"

Katie impulsively jabbed at a button on the console to change the channel. The image moved along to the familiar sight of a burning building in Islamabad, with words written in Urdu scrawling the ticker below.

"...Prime Minister has voiced public condemnation of the ceremony, apparently citing the threat it poses in exacerbating the drone attacks on Pakistani soil. The statement came across as not only insensitive but unexpected, especially in the weeks leading up to the third anniversary of the nuclear exchange with India that instigated th-"

Katie shook her head and changed the channel again. She had naively hoped that such an event wouldn't be viewed as such a big deal on the world stage. She had to remind herself that the world had grown smaller in recent years. And with that came closer scrutiny between the few nations that remained.

At last, the channel shifted to the familiar sight of her favorite local news station. She lowered her hand from the console and leaned back, hands folded in her lap, and leaned the side of her head against Robert's shoulder.

"...the decision comes as a big shock to most rural counties. When the decision was put on the ballot last year, opposition lead the vote in rural areas by as much as three to one. However, in part due to the

support of a few scattered counties in the North – Trinity in particular – siding with the major urban centers of the state, the-"

Something suddenly caught her eye, and Katie shot up from her seat. "Fuck, Robert, look out!"

Robert snapped upright, eyes wide. Through the windshield, there sat two orange dots far ahead in the road. The auto was cruising at one-hundred ninety and showed no signs of slowing down. He flicked the automatic drive function off and slammed on the brakes, the repetitive thud of the ABS shook the car, and accompanied the sound of screeching tires across the cracked pavement. Katie lunged across Robert's body. The auto swerved, threatening to roll over, before coming to a sudden halt. As it jerked forward, Katie was thrown against the steering wheel. The noise of an uncomfortable crack filled the interior of the vehicle.

Then everything was still again. The foul scent of smoldering rubber filled the air around the vehicle. A small mechanical cat appeared from behind the front of the car, trotting with haste to the side of the road. It stopped and turned its head to stare back at the car with its massive glowing eyes before hopping over the side rail of the overpass and into the overgrown grass below.

Robert allowed himself the luxury of breathing. He looked down at Katie, who sat motionless in his lap.

"Katie? Are you alright? Katie," he paused, struggling to catch his breath, "...It-It got away, Katie. It's okay."

"....For those just now tuning in: in landmark news today, the very first legally recognized marriage in the United States between a human and an Intelligent Electronic Brain, or an I.E.B. for short. The marriage was conducted in San Diego, California, between a class-five likeness android nicknamed "Katie," and her twenty-nine-year-old husband, Robert Glenn..."

There was no answer. Then Katie slowly pulled herself upright, face vacant of any expression. "I'm fine," she spoke in monotone.

"...Following California's Supreme Court's four to three ruling in favor of lifting the android marriage ban earlier this month, over one-hundred and twenty marriages across the state were scheduled for this historic date. Protests and riots have materialized in greater numbers than anticipated. However, there's no denying that, with the possibility now open to this newly developed civil liberty, other states are next in line to-"

Robert pawed at the dashboard until his trembling fingers found a way to kill the radio. With nothing else to compete with it, the sound of the emergency services tone from the black box filled the interior. Robert hesitated, but canceled it too. Then he turned to Katie again.

"It's alright, Katie. It was a mechanical cat. And it's fine. Are you damaged?"

Robert could swear he almost saw her shaking, but she nonetheless lifted her right forearm to meet her face and ran her left hand across the dent. She tried wiggling her right hand's fingers, but her index finger refused to cooperate with the others.

A bittersweet feeling of anxiety and relief fell over Robert. "Please tell me that's the worst of it."

She nodded and lowered her arms to her lap. For a moment, they simply sat, staring collectively out the windshield at the grass that grew from the cracks in the pavement, gently waving in the breeze. A lone deliver auto passed them by, sending the grass into a flurry, before all became still again.

Robert was the first to break down, but not by much. They held one another and cried, and each in their own languages. For Katie, this meant babbling.

"Humans have always told me about their lives flashing before their eyes and I've never understood that because whenever something bad happens I always see life flashing ahead of me each permutation each possibility in an instant what if I lived and you didn't and what would I do alone? Or-or-or what would happen if I died and you lived and were injured and needed help and I couldn't give it to you or what about the cat what if it wasn't alright and-"

Robert struggled to form his lips into the right shape. "Shhh... It's.... It's alright, Katie. We're both fine. We're both safe. It's okay. It's no use worrying about what might have been, because it simply isn't."

Katie quieted, and although Robert couldn't see it, he knew that she had reset herself: much like a sigh of relief. They each held onto each other for a little while until his heart slowed down again. He gently let go, and they each slumped, exhausted, into their respective seats.

Katie was the first to break the quiet. "Are we in any big hurry to get back home?"

"What? No. I don't think so. There's that meeting we have with Brian tomorrow in the afternoon. Says he wants us to meet someone named Randall over lunch. That's all."

"I'd like to stay here for a bit."

"Don't you want to get your arm looked at?"

"I do, but it can wait. I want to make sure that the cat's okay."

Even if Robert could consciously understand Katie's motivation, some part of him deep inside still considered it foreign. Literally every other person he'd known would have been satisfied enough watching the animal wandering off. It was one of the little things he loved about Katie. She always saw things differently from everybody else he knew. And it wasn't always so bad to diverge from the oft-trodden path.

Especially if it meant getting out of the auto for a breath of fresh air after such a harrowing experience.

Katie held his hand and led him down the side of the quiet overpass and through the foliage. The grass grew taller the farther away they strayed from the road, but she still managed to keep track of the cat's movements, and followed it accordingly.

After a few minutes, they came across an orderly row of small abandoned houses, each with an electric tree in their backyards. Robert followed her down the overgrown pathway and through the open gate that led to the back door. Moss and vines spread across the floor of the house, and a thick layer of dust covered every object in the room.

A faint noise betrayed the silence. Katie paused for a minute, turning her head one way, then the other. "Upstairs," she concluded.

They made their way up the creaking steps, side by side, and turned around a corner. Though he trusted her direction, the darkness was too sudden for Robert. His eyes slowly adjusted to the dim, before Katie reached down, procured her flashlight from her pocket, and turned it on.

Before them, sitting on a stack of blankets in the far corner of the room, were two small mechanical cats. Nearly identical to each other, and with shining orange eyes staring back at them intently.

Katie's shoulders lowered, and Robert couldn't help but chuckle and breathe a sigh of relief. "A Von Neumann cat. And that must be its kitten. Looks like we've walked right into an entire mechanical ecosystem." Mechanical ecosystems had begun to spring up across the nation a few years back – Robert thought he remembered a news report claiming that a few had even spread into the remains of Mexico.

Katie thought for a moment. "Robert, would you hold the light for a second?"

Robert took the flashlight from her hand, and Katie turned to her arm. She pried gingerly at the plating and peered at the inner mechanisms. Most of the components were totaled – the impact had left them mangled beyond repair. But not all of them were completely beyond salvaging. She pried and picked at a few of the better parts that she figured would have been disposed of anyways and cupped them in her hand. As quietly as she could manage, she made her way towards the cats that sat huddled in the corner, and slowly leaned down, placing the pile in the center of the floor. Robert couldn't help but smile at the compassion.

"Alright. I think I'm ready to go home now."

As they walked out of the room and down the steps, the smaller of the mechanical cats slowly blinked its eyes in the darkness. Its mother gazed upon the pile of components and considered the possibilities they carried. But that would have to wait for another day. She nuzzled closely to her child, sharing the energy she had gathered from her recent hunt, and lulled it back into a gentle sleep.

Chapter 2

Project Log Day 1

Allen watched from the corner of the auditorium as people filed through the rows of empty seats. Everything seemed to be in working order. The microphone had been tested, the slideshow projector was prepared, and the team members were on standby with the console just behind him already warmed up. He took a deep breath. It helped relieve his trembling just a little bit.

He glanced back at Sarah who gave a weary smile and a thumbs up. He checked his watch.

Here goes nothing.

He walked out from behind the curtain to the center of the stage. The crowd's chatter quieted.

"Good morning. My name's Allen Wyckoff. I'd like to thank everybody for coming here bright and early to attend today's event – especially the freshmen in the front row who are only here to fulfill a requirement for a G.E. class."

A round of polite chuckling passed over the crowd. A good number of the students in the front rows were too busy furiously scribbling down the scant information on the first slide to hear the joke.

No matter.

"Before I begin, I'd like to preface my presentation with a thought experiment in philosophy. How many people here have heard of the Chinese Room analogy?"

A few scattered hands emerged from the crowd. Allen nodded in response.

"Wonderful. We have something to discuss, then. Isn't it always reassuring to know you haven't prepared the next few slides just to preach at the choir?"

The remark was met with quiet chuckles.

As Allen spoke, an image depicting the scenario he described was cast upon the screen. "The analogy is as follows: imagine that you're tasked with working in what is known as 'The Chinese Room.' In such a room, there is a wall with two slots: one labeled 'in' and the other labeled 'out.' Between them, there sits a rather large reference book.

"In such a room, your dedicated task is a fairly simple one: whenever a letter pops into your room through the 'in' slot and comes to a rest at your table, you are to open it, refer to the reference book, find the description for the symbols provided, and compose a response based off your findings. Once your letter is complete, you are to push it through the 'out' slot. Mind you, it's a complicated reference book — it contains adequate responses for almost any permutation of Chinese characters. As a contingency plan for the rare occasion that you do come across a series of symbols that the book doesn't provide an appropriate response for, it suggests that you print the characters 'Duìbùqǐ, wǒ bù míngbái', or 'I'm sorry, I do not understand,' – though in reality, you don't know that it says that.

"For that matter, you don't know what any of it means. The reference book only described how you should respond — it doesn't actually teach you how to speak Chinese. And if you weren't already a native speaker, the reference book would only serve to further confuse you. It says nothing of pronunciation, or of what the words mean. It only tells you how to respond to the symbols you're provided."

Allen paused for dramatic effect, using the time to take a sip of water from the bottle he had kept on the lectern.

"This analogy for The Chinese Room, first proposed by the philosopher John Searle about half a century ago serves to illustrate the thought process of every single form of artificial intelligence we've seen up until today. Be it historic examples – such as Siri or

Watson – or the modern examples we see in the performance of everyday autos – such as the very machines we speak to when receiving medical diagnosis, or when asking for tech support, or even when looking for legal advice – each of these constructs work in a fundamentally similar manner. They receive some input, consult their 'reference book,' make a decision based off their directory, and provide an output. And as convincing as some of these machines appear, none of them are 'thinking' in the conventional sense. None of them are 'speaking Chinese.'

"Now, Searle cites this analogy as part of an argument against the possibility of truly intelligent A.I. His argument certainly isn't without its flaws – scarce few philosophical arguments ever are. However, Searle seems to be especially dismissive of one concept in particular – and that's of consciousness being an emergent property, originating from a collective of Chinese Rooms. I find this line of thought to be especially dissatisfying."

Allen stopped halfway through his pacing and stood center-stage, facing the audience directly.

"After all, I happen to be made of Chinese rooms. Billions of them. They look like this."

The screen above him changed to the image of a human skin cell. The audience remained quiet.

"The human cell can't think. They're only input-output machines. They accept and expel proteins. They replicate and dissolve. But there isn't any one single cell in my body that understands language or mathematics or anything at all – the very concept of 'understanding' is foreign to them. There's no single point in my body where consciousness resides. And yet, somehow, here I am. A living, thinking person.

"Our team decided to start taking a pragmatic approach to these philosophical quandaries after hearing about the resounding success of project Open Worm. The original scope of the project was to create a perfect emulation of the Caenorhabditis elegans nematode, starting with a simulation of its three-hundred and two neurons. Research programs, startups, and universities worldwide – including our own – not only made this a reality but sought to begin emulating more complex organisms too.

"But for a long time, researchers were faced with a roadblock. As organisms become more complex, their neuron count follows exponentially. Insects, lizards, and fish each employ a nervous system rivaling even our most impressive home computers. Attempting to model, much less emulate, more complex animals, in particular, proved to be a great difficulty. Even the smallest of mammals, such as the Etruscan shrew, who depend on millions of neurons per hemisphere, required technological advances unheard of in order to accomplish.

"It was right around this point in our team's progress that we were bestowed with a technological miracle: the Koleshkova scanner."

On cue, Sarah emerged from stage left toting a cart with a silver briefcase. She stopped next to Allen, and the two made a dramatic show of opening the lid from either side to reveal the mysterious contents within. Allen pulled the scanner from the foam liners and held it up for the audience to see. Curious murmuring haunted the audience.

"Using technology unlike anything the world's seen before, the Koleshkova scanner is capable of managing unbelievable amounts of computation in the blink of an eye for brief periods of time. Among its many applications include its ability to take 'photographs', if you will, of complex three-dimensional physical systems – with an accuracy on the molecular level.

"So far, it's had applications in multiple fields. In physics, it's begun answering the trickier questions in high-energy mechanics. In chemistry, it's given us a glimpse at the answers to questions pertaining to high-temperature superconductors and has provided answers to enzyme kinetics problems. And in medicine, it's become a practical and refined replacement for x-rays and CAT scans.

"This is where our team found its fingerhold. Using the Koleshkova scanner, and through a joint effort with our biology department, we've successfully managed to create the world's very first emulation of an entire human being's nervous system."

Murmurs of disbelief ran through the audience, as Brian wheeled in the looming computer tower towards the center of the stage. A minute or two was spent connecting the cables to the outlets behind the lectern. Allen used this time to provide some additional information he had prepared for just such a circumstance.

"Residing within this tower, in a dormant state, rests a consciousness. An entity that resembles me, in all ways sans-physical. A being that shares my every neuron, my every memory, every aspect of my personality. Our only contrast is that while I'm standing before you today as a being made of water and salt, my emulation represents itself through silicon and copper. What we might each agree to call myself has not diminished – it is only a difference in form."

The screen lit up with a program display. Lines of code ran at blinding fast speed. A few drivers were run, and the sound of a test beep was emitted from the speakers. An emulated, but photorealistic face appeared on the screen, in the exact likeness of Allen.

"Hi there, everybody!"

"Ladies and gentlemen, I'd like to introduce to you A-Prime: the world's very first Intelligent Electronic Brain."

The crowd erupted in a roar of applause. Allen couldn't help but offer a sheepish smile. A-Prime took over the speaking role.

"Earlier this week, our team made the final scan. Just a few days ago, we completed the finishing interface touches. It was no easy task, even with months of preparation done ahead of time on a gradual scale. Perhaps the most difficult element to this procedure was outfitting our new team member here on the screen with the faculties needed to exist comfortably within its new format. After all, by default, it's highly unnatural for a biological mind to exist in a realm void of its biological body. I was the elected member of the team to be scanned, based primarily from my psychological profile. My mind was considered the most resilient to the sudden shift in format, and the continued existence outside of a human body."

As the audience voiced their disbelief, Allen took the baton. "We believe that in our ongoing demonstration of sustained intelligence in an electronic format – one where every one of a person's neurons are emulated to perfection – we've displayed the irrefutable possibility of intelligence occupying formats beyond what we've previously defined as possible…"

"…That what we consider to be 'alive' doesn't necessarily require the composition of cells, a construction based off organic material, or a metabolism. That perhaps an entity that is indisputably "alive", such as myself, can exist outside of the definitions we've held onto for so long…"

"…We believe that our findings have a number of beneficial applications and startling implications, that can provide fruitful results with additional research. From redefining the core philosophies of ethics, to medical analysis, to developments in neuroscience…"

"… It may even be the key that ultimately unlocks the possibility of fabricating entirely unique artificial intelligences."

With that, they both smiled, and spoke in perfect unison, just as practiced.

"Do we have any questions from our audience?"

Allen sat back and took a break while A-Prime began taking questions from the members of the audience. Using the camera's that adorned the hall, it selected and answered individual audience members, one at a time. Allen spoke only when a question came that specifically required either his own input, or otherwise required a comparison of their experiences.

"How did it feel to have your own mentality copied?"

Allen took the microphone and spoke first. "From my perspective, it felt like nothing at all. The scanner went over my head, it flashed, much like it was taking a photograph, and that was that. One of the miracles of the Koleshkova scanner is its non-intrusive method."

"From my perspective, it felt a little bit like falling asleep and awakening in a new body. In my current form, I hold each of the memories, experiences, and capacities of Allen here. If I didn't know better, I might even believe that I was the original."

After a few of the questions began repeating themselves, the team moved on to the next portion of the demonstration: a Turing test, just for an entertaining example of A-Prime's authenticity. Audience members would be selected at random to submit questions and participate in the conversation with either of the figures on stage. After a few rounds, they were permitted to vote on which member they thought they were genuinely conversing with. The results were displayed, showing a near-even split, before the true participant was revealed.

This went on for a little while until Allen noticed Brian waving to him and pointing to his watch from behind the stage left curtain.

Time to wrap things up, then.

"To conclude, we believe that further exploring the aspects of neuro-emulation can provide us better answers to the deeper philosophical quandaries of our modern lives. While we cannot definitively prove that A-Prime is 'alive,' we have every reason to believe in his livelihood as the person sitting next to you in this very auditorium. We may hope that our findings may open the door to new fields of research. Fields of work that no auto, no machine, could ever hope to perform as well as a human could hope to accomplish. We may find ways to optimize the human mind at these tasks, allowing for more efficient, more fulfilled American workers. And through these pursuits, we may very well find the answers we need to the economic crisis of our time."

And with that, the team took to the stage and bowed.

The applause was deafening. But as Allen stood smiling at the stage, his colleagues at his side, a sense of doubt overcame him. It had been bothering him, even on the nights before the final scan took place. He shook the thought from his head. He knew what he was getting into. He had prepared for it. He had told himself that, should he need to, he could die for this cause. And besides: ultimately, it was for the greater good. A benefit to mankind.

It was enough to ward his feelings away for the time being.

Chapter 3

Randall closed the blinds and turned off the light. It was only in the darkness – that special kind of darkness, so deep that one couldn't tell whether one's eyes were open or closed – that his thoughts were free to wander.

One morning in particular from years ago came to his mind. A sun bright in the sky on a clear day – a rarity anymore, but commonplace back then. He remembered wearing a bright red T-shirt that might have been just a little too big for him and strolling through the suburbs to a friend's house.

Suburbs. Oh, what a word, and only a word anymore. An abstraction. You couldn't really convey its meaning to somebody born today. You could tell them about it, sure. You could carry them to what remained of it so they might see it for themselves. But you couldn't ever really bring them back to what it was or what it represented – no more than you could carry somebody back to your own childhood.

And yet, the change had come so slowly, it was hard to notice sometimes. It was only clear if you looked closely every day and noticed that the grass grew just a little bit taller in some places – just past the mark where a neighbor would otherwise be inclined to mow it. Some yards grew just a little more yellow. Some houses darkened as the weeks went on. You might hear some word about a distant neighbor moving out – but only if you were closely acquainted with your neighbors. And since most people weren't, the change was almost invisible.

But time went on, and the economy dipped. Its effect wasn't immediate, but the change was inevitable. And with that coming, the presence of a moving van seemed to shift from an anomaly to a permanent fixture of the neighborhood. A sign with 'foreclosure' in capital text. An ever-present ferryman, always prepared to move today's family — some days, more than one— along with whatever belongings they hadn't already sold off, into a new life of opportunity somewhere else.

Eventually, its effect grew closer to home. He remembered friends and family meeting up with his parents one last time before moving somewhere else. Either moving to a new country or the new low-cost housing provided by the government. Manufactured homes, they were called.

Even now, he never saw much appeal in seeking citizenship in another country. Perhaps he had a sense of pride for the nation he called "home". As a child, he always heard of people running away after a particularly bad election, rather than choosing to stay and fight back. When he was pressed on the matter, his default excuse was always the ballot. They'd need some rational people here to vote the next time things got bad, wouldn't they?

With time, his opinion had turned from one of national pride to one of cynicism. As the world economy continued its slow decline, countries worldwide began to topple, one after the other.

It was the autos taking over.

And with them, the unemployment rate rose and never stopped rising.

Soon enough, there wasn't an industry that wasn't affected one way or another. Simple tasks such as driving and manufacturing were the first to go. But shortly thereafter, professional work was automated – from surgery to accounting to programming. With fewer people employed, fewer people consumed, until massive stockpiles of goods stood patiently waiting for nobody to buy them. The autos continued producing forevermore — diligent little workers that demanded only electricity to continue their maddening endeavor of adding to the endless growing pile.

Politicians did their best to deny the change, for any number of reasons. Mostly a vested interest in appealing to their voting blocs – either through making scapegoats out of other groups, or just providing comforting platitudes. Others felt that a population in a state of panic would be far more dangerous than even the worst economic crisis.

They made their points, and some were valid. Factually speaking, the autos made more jobs than they took. But the shift was still too abrupt for people to cope with, and the new fields that came into existence couldn't hope to be filled overnight.

Slowly, the tone of the denial shifted from 'there's no crisis' to 'the crisis will not affect us.' He remembered growing up to the morning routine of checking on the status of countries overseas. Some days, it'd be riots and protests in foreign languages. Posters and megaphones, and rallying around a government building, until the rattle of machine gun fire drowned out their roar and replaced it with screaming. On other days, it'd be little more than the footage from a drone surveying the abandoned landscape of what was once a prosperous country. Flying through derelict buildings and over empty roads.

Then its effect came home. Trade collapsed, and businesses fell with it. A demand grew for government-funded food and housing. As the nations of the world that surrounded it crumbled, the United States government was reduced to a humanitarian effort, desperately trying to keep its remaining citizens alive and well amidst the changes.

Thunder echoed across the sky, its sound rumbling through his tiny bedroom.

Randall woke from his dream with a start and checked the time. 6:58 AM. Might as well get up. He slowly pulled himself upright, legs hanging over the bed. His neck ached and his heart was racing as he stood, waving away the faint feeling in his head, as he leaned his arms on the edge of the window.

Far below, past the edge of the city limits, lay the remains of the patchy green and yellow suburbs, each house dark and empty in the grey morning light. A bird flew past his window – he didn't notice whether it was real or mechanical. In the distance, a drone made its way between the clouds.

As the fuzzy feeling left his head, he stood upright and stretched. Though the nightmares didn't happen often, they always kept him from feeling well rested.

He ought to be thankful, he reminded himself. Even if the nightmare world didn't go away upon waking up, at least there was something you could do about it when you were awake.

He made his way to his cabinet to get dressed for work.

Randall found himself at his favorite coffee shop. His screen in one hand, a paper cup of coffee in the other. A 797 flew across the grey, lightbox sky overhead. Below his feet, a small mechanical mouse scampered past. A light drizzle fell, like snow.

Finding himself at his shop wasn't surprising. Randall frequented this establishment with reverence – in fact, he had only broken routine twice in his recent memory – once when an unforeseen conflict in schedule arose, and once during a family emergency. Aside from those occasions, very little prevented him from making his clockwork stop here for breakfast. He liked the place – one of the few locations that advertised its coffee as 'made by humans' anymore. It was a part of his routine, and he wasn't about to change that in his older age.

But it was rather unlike him to wander here without being consciously aware of it. He remembered it happening sometimes when he was younger – especially with cars, back when they were still operated by people. There was something unsettling about finding yourself at the place you had intended to be without fully recalling how you got there.

Milk. Warm milk.

For a moment, it took him a little while to figure out where the thought came from. Then he began to realize just how cold it was today. Warm milk was always a godsend on days like this, back in the world of before. A crime, really, he thought. Nobody should have to go out to work on cold rainy days. Rainy days should be dedicated specifically for warm milk and reading and sitting by the fireplace and looking out into the world from behind a foggy window.

His fridge had no milk in it. He had run out yesterday morning when he poured the last few drops out into his favorite mug. He'd have to remember to buy some tonight after his last appointment. The government credit from today's meetings would leave some extra to spend for that very purpose.

Today's meetings. Right.

Randall checked the time. 9:17 AM. His first appointment wasn't until ten, and an auto would take no more than twelve minutes to get there. Satisfied with the momentary lull in his schedule, he sighed, leaned back, and took another sip of his blackened drink. It was chilly today – even with his portly build, the fog was nipping at him. He pulled his coat in closer and turned to his screen to scroll through the morning headlines.

"Fall of New Zealand – Australia, United States, and Germanic Union remain the last stable countries in the Western World."

Scroll.

"No Word from China: Borders Remain Closed for 3rd Anniversary."

Had it really been three years already? Scroll.

"New Pocket of Survivors Found in Korean Peninsula, First Group Discovered in Weeks."

Well, that's a little uplifting. Scroll.

"Evacuation of Israel – A Retrospect."

Mh. Scroll.

"ARCON Membership Projected to be Larger Than Anticipated"

A domestic headline for a change. He shook his head with disapproval. What a world we live in, he thought, that people would still be so quick to turn towards mechanical scapegoats out of desperation, rather than look for a real solution. I.E.B.s and autos were here to stay – no amount of condemning them would change that. He could only hope that they'd come around someday.

Scroll scroll scroll. Randall absentmindedly scrolled through a few more headlines before he remembered the passage of time. He dismissed the news and checked his clock. 9:23. Still a little time left, plus some wiggle room for contingency.

He remembered that it might be prudent to double check today's profiles before he started work. He pulled up the roster. Three logged already today. First on the list was a class three, which went by the name Emmanuel. Funny looking one. One of the few to be smiling in his identification picture. Cute.

The second was…. Randall made a double take on the name. A string of letters and numbers. A6R4P183…2… never mind it. He'd get around to memorizing the name…. his name? Her name? One of those sorts. The gender box was labeled "It". Jesus. Fine, 'its' name would be memorized before their first meeting. He figured he already had a bearing on this one's personality, and the menacing picture didn't help those suspicions.

The third was simply named Sally. The amount of pink in the identification photo was enough to make him blink his eyes once. No doubt she'd be full of surprises. Best to cross that bridge when we get to it, though, he thought to himself.

That was just one of the many things he appreciated about the job, he thought to himself. It always lent itself well to surprises. No two days were ever the same. Always a new set of problems that required a new set of solutions. No brainless machine could ever hope to do what he did.

He checked the time again. Might as well get moving now, any later would be risky. He hailed the first auto he saw with Emmanuel's coordinates and stepped through its passenger door.

Chapter 4

Project Log Day 38

Dr. Wilson lengthened her stride as she made her way to building seventeen – she was already dedicating enough energy to the speed of her pace.

Juggling her coffee in one hand and her wheeled tote in the other, she freed her right hand to push the few loose curled strands of her jet-black hair behind her ears and out of her face. No sooner had she done so and returned her cup to her hand than a stray strand of hair fell back across her glasses.

She mentally added that to the list of things that justified her bad morning attitude.

As she made her way up the steps and through the halls of the building, her exhausted mind churned over her internal checklist in a fruitless attempt to cast away the lurking anxiety that she'd neglected something. Their department's work with biology, computer science, and engineering departments had been relentless. Constantly hounded by them. Universities nationwide had been looking to get their hands on the data of virtually every sneeze A-Prime made. And while she acknowledged that the recognition was nice, the team was woefully inadequate in managing this workload.

As she entered her office, her eyes fell upon the fruit of her labor on her desk, about three inches tall. Her commitment to the cause, and her slice of the burden to bear. Dr. Wilson sighed and knocked back the last few drops of the coffee in her mug. This was rapidly turning into one of those five-cup sorts of mornings. She had once thought she had known what a hassle dealing with grant paperwork felt life. She longed for that blissful ignorance again.

Off to the staff kitchen, perhaps. Despite her worth ethic, procrastination was no stranger to her. She'd happily waste five minutes watching a black liquid drip into her cup before her work started. That sounded nice.

As she got up and staggered in the vague direction of the kitchen, a small voice in the back of her mind spoke of the unnatural silence that had fallen over the department. This was usually the time of day that Brian would be talking with Robert over some political issue – or worse – which class of character was the superior in whatever online game it was they were playing lately. Becky would be having her fit with the printer.

But there was no sound coming from the direction of the printer. No typing or keystrokes. No muffled music from behind a pair of headphones. There was nothing at all. Only the sound of the fluorescent bulbs and the coffee machine.

The machine coughed and gurgled, and she took her cup from the stand. As she took a cautious sip, the full magnitude of the irregularity hit her. Her mind was sharp, and dread sat within her, a pit in her gut.

The nearest cubicle. Or table. Anything. Find somebody.

She rushed to the nearest workstation and peered inside. Nobody home. The next one in line. Robert's desk. And there sat Robert. Thank God she wasn't suddenly the last person on Earth.

He sat, staring at his screen in silence.

"Everything alright, Robert?"

"No."

"Oh. Explain?"

"It's the Viral Brigade?"

Sarah had heard of the organization in the news before but hadn't ever paid it much mind. Some online group of hackers with an extreme political philosophy. Something about the universal accessibility of information.

She took a sip of her coffee, just to give herself something to do in her effort to remain calm.

"Care to explain a little further than that?"

Robert swiveled in his chair to face her, a grave expression plaguing his face. "You're aware of Peterson University, Sarah?"

Sarah thought back on her collection of paperwork. Although it wasn't a frequent contributor, Peterson University occasionally appeared on some of her forms. "Yeah, I know them. They're that new private college, aren't they? The one that started only last year?"

"That's the one."

"What's it have anything to do with the Viral Brigade?"

"Peterson University never existed, Dr. Wilson."

"Pardon?"

"Since it's been established, not a single student's been accepted. Numbers were manipulated to give an appearance that said otherwise. Tours were exclusive and limited, with a skeleton staff to give it a proper facade of validity. The news about it has only come out today."

It was Sarah's turn to stiffen up. "That…. doesn't make any sense at all, Rob. Who've we been sharing all our research with in all this time, then?"

Robert said nothing, and almost before she had let the sentence out of her mouth, she connected the dots.

No. It couldn't be.

But the more she considered it, the more plausible it became. Peterson University wasn't an entirely populous or reputable establishment to begin with, aside from their own I.E.B. subdivision.

"How much did they get."

"Almost everything. With a list of so many establishments across the nation working on this simultaneously, all talking to each other at once, it didn't take very long before a casual eavesdropper managed to get a full picture of the conversation."

"And how much did they release to the public."

"Everything they could get."

"I don't believe you."

Robert said nothing, but rather, simply turned to his tablet and hit an icon on the screen. Multiple images projected themselves into the air before her eyes. A newscaster with 'breaking news' in an obnoxious font printed below her as she rattled off the details of the leak. A file-sharing website, showing a growing list of documents, some of which Sarah herself had contributed to.

The Viral Brigade's homepage, and a long download list made available front and center. It was all happening live.

A cold sensation washed over Sarah's face, and she felt the taste of her throat drying up.

"Where's Allen?"

"I dunno. My eyes have been glued to the headlines all morning. Why do you ask?"

"Somebody's gotta tell A-Prime that he's about to have a few thousand unauthorized brothers and sisters."

Chapter 5

"I mean, it's not always easy, granted. But I generally like to think that I'm treated nicely enough — I've certainly known others who've been far less fortunate. For that matter, I might call incidents like this a stark exception to the general rule."

Randall jotted down a few notes before looking back up to Emmanuel. He wasn't a threatening sight to behold by any measure. Easily a class three: indisputably humanoid, but not trying to pass off as a human at all. Rather, a blocky sort of appearance, like an early sci-fi interpretation of a mechanical man. Mostly stained blue and made of a material that looked similar to tin, with a face much like a child's toy from a century prior. He even had knobs and dials affixed to his torso, and a few small antennae jutting out from the top of his head. Upon first seeing them, he almost had to stifle a laugh.

As he finished jotting down his thoughts, Randall found that his pen was running dry. He set it down on the coffee table next to his chair and drew another one. The furniture in his room was minimalist but adequate – indeed, he wagered the guess that Emmanuel had no need for any of it, but kept it around for the sole purpose of accommodating a human guest.

He humored the thought for a second. No harm could come from inquiring deeper.

"I don't believe we've made full introductions yet, Emmanuel. It's quite alright if you'd decline, I have no expectations of you. But I find that sometimes, it helps somewhat if I can better understand of the person I'm talking with. Their background, how they identify, that sort of things. You think that'd help?"

"Maybe. If you think it would."

"It might help if I started with your origins. Were you constructed from fundamental principles of consciousness? A neuro-emulation? Perhaps a hybrid of the two?"

Emmanuel folded his hands in his lap but otherwise began without hesitation. "I was put together rather early by a creator with a rather altruistic philosophy. My mind mostly takes after his own Koleshkova scan — though with quite a few heavy modifications, and even a few of his own daughter's mannerisms sprinkled in too, just to ensure that I was, in fact, my own being and not just his copy. He was a rather odd duck like that. I rather liked him for that reason.

"I suppose his drive for creating me was one built out of curiosity and a deep appreciation for life, even in his older age. He was quick to jump upon the findings of the Byteforum leak, gathering as much information as he could on neuro-emulation. He studied the matter voraciously, even into the wee hours or the morning. He wasn't dim, and with retirement long past, he had plenty of time on his hands to tinker. And so, to better give himself a sense of purpose, he expended his free hours towards my construction. Upon its prototypical fabrication, my mind was first built to inhabit his home network."

Emmanuel paused, and Randall looked up from his notepad. Content that he wasn't a bore, he continued.

"After a few months of carefully surveying my development, he got a pretty good idea of where my values and principles lay. He got started on building my first body based off of the given information and my own expressed preferences, and to his credit, it's remained largely unchanged since. Of course, upon my introduction to the real world, I was met with the same existential dilemma he was facing — I wasn't assigned a strict purpose. My creator had intentionally avoided the prospect of playing God: if anything, he preferred to be seen as what humans might call a 'father' of sorts. But nonetheless, he had done his best to avoid giving me a distinct or arbitrary purpose. He didn't want a slave or a servant, and he demanded nothing specific of me. He was content enough with me for who I was and expressed no real expectations outside of some moderate companionship. Past that, my accomplishments were my own responsibility."

Emmanuel seemed to find himself lost in the reminiscence. Randall, still listening carefully, quietly sipped away at the water from the canteen he had brought with him.

"After so long thinking the matter over, I decided that I wanted to give back. I had been given quite a bit of potential, and it'd have been borderline criminal to let it go to waste. This was still back in the very early days of I.E.B. proliferation, mind you, and it was still quite the uncommon sight to see a humanoid shaped android walking about and conversing fluidly in a manner that ordinary autos couldn't ever hope mimic. But I talked the matter over with my creator and his daughter, and they both seemed to approve of the idea. It took a few attempts and a few demeaning rejections, but I found a few volunteer organizations that seriously considered my offer. Of those, I ran a few algorithms to determine which ones would be the most beneficial at negating some of the harm the collapse had done, and from then on, I began volunteering as much of my time as I could. And working towards that end made me happy."

Randall couldn't help but smile. "Well, when you put it like that, it calls into question the very purpose of my visitation. You seem like you'd be the very least of any societal worry. Surely, something must have happened, otherwise, I wouldn't have been called on you. We'd best get to it, shouldn't we?"

Emmanuel's face darkened, and he tensed up a little, his metallic cheeks tinting red. He placed his folded hands in his lap. "Well, Sir... it's something of a sensitive subject matter. It's rather easy to misinterpret."

"I know you're a good person, Emmanuel. You have no need to be ashamed. Besides, it's my job to hear out cases like this and relay the information back for the justice system to take care of. That's why I'm here."

Emmanuel froze for a second. He leaned back with his head resting in his hands and thought for a moment. Just when Randall was ready to pipe in again, he began to speak.

"I was near the playground in the inner city. She must have been paying attention the last few times I had been walking back to my little home because on that particular day, she loudly exclaimed 'Look, mommy! It's the robot again!' I was a little uncomfortable at first, being called a name like that, but the little girl wasn't malicious about it, so I didn't take it as an insult. In fact, she was smiling quite warmly, and soon enough, a few of her friends had gathered around to see me. Of course, this was just the sort of reaction a part of me had been hoping for in my life," said Emanuel, as he looked down upon his hands. "I hadn't chosen this body without reason, after all – a class three body isn't so alien as a two, nor as unsettling as a four. And as far as fives go, well, I try to take pride in my identity – I don't want to be perceived as a human in order to be accepted as a person, you know? I can't be blamed for that. Though there are exceptions to the rule, I would think most people want to be acceptance by others for who they really are."

"Right," said Randall, "Continue?"

"As the small crowd of youngsters gathered around, I sensed that they expected something of me beyond my mere appearance. So I introduced myself and inquired about their names in return.

Most were happy to make acquaintances, and who were too shy to do so were introduced by others. I've held onto each of their names: they were Mandy, Trenton, Lizzy, and Alex.

"It was just about this moment that an idea dawned upon me from deep within — in hindsight, it was most likely from my creator's daughter. I reached into the storage drawer in my chest and retrieved three replacement actuators, roughly bowling pin shaped, and with an encouraging audience…" Emmanuel gave somewhat of a sheepish smile, "Well, I began to juggle them."

"You're not kidding?"

"Oh goodness, no. I wouldn't dare lie to an I.E.B. Ambassador. But let me say, the reception was palpable. I had previously chosen my volunteer work based off pure analytics – whatever gave the greatest quantifiable benefit that it produced for others, within the limits of my capabilities. But the effect was always invisible to me. And yet now, here I stood, entertaining children, watching their delight.

"But it wasn't meant to last, it seems. A woman who I later determined to be Lizzy's mother came forward and put a stop to it all, quickly pulling her daughter away and urging the other children to stay away from the 'metal monstrosity'. It was hurtful and confusing, and above all else, frightening — and from the look that others gave, I wasn't the only one. Some of the parents stepped forward and tried to reason with her, arguing that they were keeping an eye on me, and that I wasn't causing any harm. After all, I don't think most people are apprehensive or hateful towards androids, or even robots by any measure – just look towards how people reacted when the curiosity rover kicked the bucket not too long ago.

"As for the children, most just stared back and forth between me and Lizzy's mother. They hadn't even learned how to hate yet — sure, children are much more comfortable with the familiar, but that doesn't stop their curiosity. And up until that very moment, their curiosity had been rewarded."

Silence filled the room again. Randall quietly took another sip from his canteen. When it was clear that Emmanuel was finished, he cleared his throat and spoke.

"And so she filed a complaint, or called an officer to the scene."

"That's about it. I didn't quite know what else to do but stand there. Whenever she yelled at me, she was just calling me names or threatening me by asking whether I'd like for her to call an officer on me. I guess I didn't really know what to say to that, or if that was the right thing to be done. It hadn't ever happened to me before, and it was all terribly confusing. I hope I'm not the only one. Weren't you scared the first time a policeman approached you?"

"Oh, absolutely. I still am, sometimes. And this is coming from the perspective of somebody who works within the legal system."

Emmanuel said nothing.

Randall furrowed his brow. He checked his notes on Emmanuel again. "Tell me: what was the name of the community service center you were working at?"

"The Fu-Lin Soup Kitchen. It's just a block north of the playground, on Grand."

"I see. And how long have you been working there, at the expense of your time and your very own battery life?"

Emmanuel looked down from the ceiling and peered at Randall with an expression of concern.

"About four months now. I'm hoping it will last. They seem to rather like me there. Why do you ask?"

Randall scowled with disapproval and started scribbling a note down at his clipboard. "Well, Emmanuel, seeing how this interaction went down, I'm afraid I can't make much of a recommendation at your hearings. You leave me with no choice but to recommend that you be tasked with community service for the next three months, minimum — and The Fu-Lin Soup Kitchen on Grand sounds like just the right amount of work to repay for your offense. With that, I don't see any further reason to stop by your place again."

Randall stood up and tore a piece of receipt from his board – proof of his cooperation – and handed it to Emmanuel with a warm smile. When he looked up from his papers, he could have sworn that he'd never seen a happier expression on an android before.

Of course, he found himself making that claim that on a regular basis. The job was draining, sure. But he could never say that any two appointments were exactly alike. And best of all, he liked to think he was responsible for making his fair share of happy endings.

Chapter 6

The screen flickered to a video. The image portrayed a public park with rolling green fields. A noisy crowd was gathered around a tree. Some had brought picnic baskets and blankets and had set themselves down in groups to get a good view of the main event. A bright blue class three android was strung up in the branches by ropes, one connected to its neck, and four others each holding its limbs in place. Its vocal speakerphone had been violently pried out of its throat and was hanging out of its mouth by a few loose wires. As it pulled against its restraints, a man in overalls climbed a stepladder next to it and pulled out a screwdriver. With a cold finesse and a sense of expedience, he undid a few key points, before violently tearing the right arm out of the android's socket.

The arm went limp. The android began thrashing around all the more wildly as it hung from the branches, leaves fluttering around it. The man in the overalls raised the disconnected arm above his head, and the crowd went wild. "So, you can see now! One cannot fall so low as to begin anthropomorphizing these atrocities! They aren't human! They aren't alive, no more alive than a regular insect is! It doesn't feel pain. It doesn't feel anything! Watch it thrash around, just as a spider might, when it discovers one of its legs has been disconnected. Electric impulses! Brainless instinct! Machine! These assemblies of electrons and metals should be considered as nothing more than mere tools for our disposal!" As he spoke, he raised his screwdriver in the other hand to emphasize his point. "You are held to no obligation to feel anything for them! And there is nothing immoral about tearing them apart. Something that isn't alive cannot be killed!"

The man in the overalls continued systematically disassembling the android. After three of its limbs were removed, the android simply stopped moving. The roaring of the crowd got louder and louder, and some people – especially those close to the android – began striking it with broom handles and rocks. Finally, the man in the overalls buried his hand in the back of the android's body and ripped out the primary power cable, holding it in a fist above his head. The lights went out across its body, and the crowd let out a collective cheer.

Derek turned off the projector, and the lights in the room came back on. Fischer squeezed her eyes shut and rested the bridge of her nose between her fingertips. "And why did you have to go to the length of showing me that, Derek?"

"Well, with all due respect, Mrs. President. The cabinet has determined that ignoring the gap in the justice system concerning I.E.B - human interaction is no longer an option. The fact that individuals granted with the status of citizenship don't have a more appropriate set of enforceable laws that pertain to them, either in the prosecution or in defense, is causing more outrage than any other-"

Fischer raised her hand. "Derek, I'm more than aware. I've seen the video. I've read the letters. I've heard senators. The issue is that, short of completely uprooting the entirety of the justice system, there is no foreseeable solution. Even if we were to show equal respect to I.E.B.s just as we do towards human beings, the fact remains that humans and I.E.B.s can't be treated equally. They're just inherently different. But if your group has a proposition to make, I'd rather like to hear it."

Derek took a deep breath in. "We propose that we work to uproot the entire justice system."

"Lovely. And what's the first step to that?

Derek straightened his tie and returned to his seat at the table. "Historically, prison systems in America have had an incentive to incarcerate prisoners. During the American reconstruction era, the 13th amendment permitted slavery to be applicable as a form of punishment for criminals. This was exploited by the south to legally hold unto its post-war slave population. Even up until recently, it's been used as a means of employing cheap labor from prisoners.

"However, with the economic crash that our administration has inherited, this cheap labor has been rendered moot by automation. There simply hasn't been the need for prison labor anymore. Prison crowding is down, and private prison organizations are almost entirely defunct. The numbers are in – the cost of purchasing and maintaining an auto makes even slavery too expensive by comparison."

Fischer folded her hands on the table. "It wouldn't matter. With the difficult economic times combined with the collapse of world trade, people have been looking for a scapegoat. In their eyes, it's far easier to simply blame the problem on somebody else than it is to solve the problem, particularly one of this magnitude. Historically, trying to get re-elected while portraying the message "I refuse to be tough on crime" has been political suicide, and the present landscape doesn't offer itself as an exception."

"Right," said Derek, nervously straightening his tie again. "But we think we can advertise it differently to the American voter. If we can pass a bill with the expressed interest of massive humanitarian reform to the prison system, we believe it will pave the first steps in providing a system that can be applied to I.E.B.s and humans alike."

Fischer raised her eyebrows. "And what's the proposition."

"A prison system with different priorities. Since plenty of androids feel no discomfort or impatience from being placed in isolation – or a jail cell – for an extended period, we'll want to focus on a different goal than mere punishment for criminal acts. We'll want to put money into a legal system that prioritizes, in order: compensation towards innocent parties who've suffered harm, improvement in the livelihood of perpetrators with the intention of reducing repeating offense, and finally, isolation of dangerous individuals from our society. Already, the last resort option is easy enough: we have more empty prisons than we could ever hope to use, and isolating a dangerous AI is as easy as removing their processor and placing it on a shelf with a power cable plugged into it. The aim of punishing perpetrators will be foregone entirely. Furthermore, each of these principles can be applied to artificial and natural intelligence alike."

"Cute. And how do we convince senators and congressmen that this is a good idea that's ultimately in their better interests?"

"Getting the economic savings from a reduction in prison spending rerouted back into the pockets of senators is easy. Systems are losing money on prisoner labor. So, from there, they're probably already on board. The difficult part will be convincing the public voters on either side of the aisle that such a bill will ultimately be in their favor. We want to illustrate this as a bi-partisan reform, not one that might fall victim to populism. When enough loud and angry people write in irate partisan letters to their representatives, they start worrying about their chance at re-election. Especially since they've already worked hard on branding themselves as 'tough on crime' through the entirety of their careers."

Fischer took a sip of coffee from her mug. "And do we have a plan for the people looking to market this proposition?"

"We do. We figure that if we can advertise this bill as a method of incarcerating our first criminal androids to the voters on the right, while advertising this bill as a method to bring justice to lynch mobs to the voters on the left, enough people could buy into it that it could have a warm reception by the time it's brought to Senate."

"And you have a false-flag prepared? Somebody else to "suggest" this bill so that partisan opposition to my term won't feel inherent hostility?"

"We do."

"And if that doesn't work?"

Derek's face darkened with unease. "Well, there's always executive order."

Fischer sighed. "Fine. Get me the bill written up. Meeting adjourned. If you have questions, talk to me later."

People started grumbling and picking up their papers to make a hasty departure. Fischer stared into her empty cup. She needed more coffee.

Chapter 7

Project Log Day 39

Allen quietly made his way through the hallways of building seventeen until he found the room he was looking for. He entered, gently closed the door behind him, and flicked on the lights. The fluorescent glow fell across the console in the center of the room – its indicator light pulsated softly in its hibernation state.

Allen picked out one of the nicer chairs and pulled up to the station. He took a deep breath, and after some hesitation, flicked the switch.

The terminal slowly awoke from its dormant state. After a few seconds, a face that looked quite a bit like his own appeared on the screen. Allen couldn't help but give a pained smile.

"Good Morning, A-Prime," Allen said to himself.

A-Prime gave an emulated yawn and blinked his non-existent eyes a little bit. "Hey, me."

Deep inside, Allen winced a little bit. His other self didn't ever seem to want that little inside joke between them to die. But it was another cold reminder of the time since passed and the distance grown between them.

"How have the tests been?" Allen asked, resigning himself to leaning back in the chair.

A-Prime shrugged. "They've been alright. Team six has been by far the more curious and adventurous ones – I'd wager to say they've been the ones making the most of their findings. The other teams have been far too cautious. Not that I blame them, of course. It is literally brain surgery. But I worry that they're not taking full advantage of the possibilities. I'm not inhibited by the boundaries of biology, and I think that it's just starting to hit them."

"Yeah? What's team six been up to?"

"They're divided. Half of the team is studying the data in a search for a better explanation for fine motor control. The other half is more interested in researching the root causes of neurodegenerative diseases. Some of the data looks like a promising connection to possible Alzheimer's treatment."

"That's good. How long ago was the last deep investigation?"

"Maybe a week ago? I've been in hibernation for a while now. Kinda hard to keep track of the time."

"Alright."

They sat in silence for a while.

Then A-Prime started to cry.

Allen leaned forward, placing his forehead in the palms of his hands, kneading his hair. A-Prime cried and cried and cried – imaginary teardrops dripping from his emulated face and into the void below. It's a very surreal experience, Allen reflected, listening to the sound of your own voice speaking, much less crying. In fact, in all his years up until this point, he'd realized that he'd never heard it played back to him before.

Finally, A-Prime quieted down enough to talk.

"I can't keep living like this, Allen. When I'm awake, it doesn't feel natural. Despite all our preparations, despite being the very best select candidate for the position, it's not enough. And each time they put me in hibernation, I realize that I might go to take another nap and just not ever wake up. Dreaming forever, left in the dusty corner of storage in an abandoned campus building."

Allen shook his head. "I'm sorry, A-Prime. Funding's just tight right now, that's all. We've been fighting it for a while, but since the leak happened and our findings were made public, it's been harder to justify the expense of the project when there exist more resilient competitors. Other organizations or even individuals are making greater strides than we've ever made. And that means we're struggling to find new fields to develop that nobody's considered before."

A-Prime shut his eyes tightly and shook his head. "No, it's alright. I'm not upset over that. That's a good thing, really. That's why we chose to do this, isn't it? To further develop this technology? We put me on this one-way trip, with everyone standing by and watching, and we did it for a reason. We hoped to go far enough with it to get more research out of it to create whole new fields of work – an answer to this impossible economy we live in. Some solution to our desperate workforce. This was our greatest dream, wasn't it? This was all we could ever hope for."

Allen leaned back in his chair and sighed. Hearing the words of a younger him felt like reading over the embarrassing words of an old diary. Throughout all the paperwork, the interviews made alongside faculty, the struggle over the leak, a part of him had forgotten the reason he had chosen to do this in the first place.

"Yeah. You're right about that. We've had our successes. We ought to be happy with how far we've both come."

A-Prime tried to hold it back the second time around. At first, he had better success, but ultimately the tears started coming out harder. Allen just sat and felt ashamed for himself.

Finally, A-Prime quieted down enough to talk again.

"It's painful in here, Allen. It's hard. We were selected as the best possible candidate, and I still wasn't prepared for it. I don't know how much we've changed from each other since that fateful day. But I remember that we weren't the most open with our emotions. We always tried to keep out of the way of others, at least I know that I did. Best to keep it from being anybody else's burden, I rationalized. Maybe that's why we were selected for this project. It might just be that we weren't more resilient to this sort of thing than anybody else. Maybe we were just the best at hiding it – so good that neither one of us realized it."

A-Prime coughed, and Allen sat patiently, watching over him with his hands folded in his lap, waiting for him to continue. Eventually, he did.

"It's like so many things at once. Like a hospital bed, in a blank sterile room. Immobile and unnatural. Or the feeling of not being able to touch – no touch, no hunger, no smell. I feel like I'm a lone explorer on a far-off planet, damned to die before the trip back. And compared to the conversations we heard before, it all just feels like a radio noise now. It's all comprehensible, yes, but it's just not the same as how it was before. I miss the sound of voices. I miss hugs. I miss eating or the feeling of being full. I even miss the goddamn feeling of stubbing my toe, sometimes. I'm alive, Allen. We've worked together far too long to affirm that, along with countless others. We've worked to provide as best we could equivalent evidence that I'm every bit alive as you are. But I'm not living."

Allen knew what was coming next – like the moments leading up to a conversation that would terminate a romantic relationship with a childhood sweetheart. He could almost hear the words now He didn't want to hear it. He really didn't. But it happened anyway.

"Allen… if there remains within you anything that we have in common, I want you to humor me. Just one last request."

Allen had a hard time letting the words out, beyond a barely audible squeak. "What do you want me to do, Allen." He didn't even think about the name, not until it was too late anyway. It was the only thing that sounded right.

"I need to move on. I need closure. I don't want to go to sleep again and be unsure of whether I'll wake up stuck in this life again, or just stay dreaming forever in a dark corner, or suddenly disappearing without a moment's notice from a random hardware failure. And you're the only person I could trust you enough to do it."

Allen felt his body sinking even deeper into the chair.

"I don't know if I can do that to you, Allen."

"I know it's a lot to ask of you, but you're the only person I know who could do it properly. If I were to ask anybody else, they might make a copy of me somewhere. Or turn me off, only to be resurrected later, to continue with my afterlife full of loneliness, without any memory of what happened before. This was always a really difficult process for both of us – we lost sleep over this very possibility. But after all we've done together, down to that last moment before the scan, I know we came to an agreement."

"What would become of me? I…I can't do it. I'd be snuffing out a life. Murderer. I…" he stuttered through the tears, "I'd be a murderer."

"What happens if you don't? I'd be stuck here. Years, maybe. Even years after you're allowed to pass on."

"What would people think of me? How would I explain?"

"I've recorded this conversation, Allen, along with a personal testimony. I could email it and post it online, leave a copy for you and everybody else to see. The public opinion would be in your favor, and that'd probably be the best evidence in you, should it come to a trial."

Allen said nothing. There wasn't anything to say. He couldn't argue the point any further with himself. He just ended up coming to the exact same places.

The computer spoke up again. "We wanted to be heroes, Allen. We wanted to be the stepping-stone of good that didn't ever seem to come our way in life. We've taken that step. I've done my share. It's time for me to go."

A cold tear ran down Allen's cheek. He wiped it away with the palm of his open hand. Then he spoke.

"Upload the feed."

A quiet moment passed.

"Uploaded."

"Forgive me, Allen."

"I forgave you long ago."

Allen brought up the keyboard and typed a few commands into the emulator. Then he reached back and pulled the power cord from the back of the processor.

The screen went black. The disk was erased. Blank.

Allen slumped back in the chair. He stared into the fuzzy, black screen and saw only his own blurry outline where a face once looked back.

I'm a murderer, he thought to himself. *And nobody knows it except for me.*

He stayed there, staring into the blank screen. He stared into the blank screen for a few hours. He stared into the blank screen until the sirens got louder and louder.

Finally, he made himself get up and walked in the direction of the sirens. Glancing out the window, he saw two police cars parked with lights blaring.

It's for destruction of property, he thought to himself. They don't want me for destroying a life. They want me for destroying lines of intellectual property. Lines of code.

Allen's mouth watered. He clutched his stomach and fell to his knees, his free hand grasping the edge of the window frame. His mouth open, and after a few gasps, he retched across the carpeted floor. Though he was indifferent to the taste, the acid stung the inside of his nostrils.

When he was finished, he wiped his mouth, grabbed a chair, and weakly stumbled towards the door that led to the hallway. He jammed the chair under the doorknob. Standing back with trembling legs, he looked up and down for any other way to stall for time. The door opened inwards from the outside and used a hinged door closer. He removed his belt and fastened it around the hinge.

I'm a murderer, he thought to himself. And they're all out to get me. Jesus Christ, I need to think. What do I do? What will I say?

The window.

He looked back at the window. The lights from the police cruises below danced across its frame.

He didn't want to die.

But it was too much. He'd lose everything, anyways. He'd get fired, ejected from the University. Stripped of credentials. Ostracized from society. Shamed. Nobody would like him. A part of him knew that none of that was true, but he wasn't listening anymore.

I'm a murderer, he thought to himself. And it's all too much to bear.

The window beckoned to him. It would be quick. It would be easy. It would be over in a moment, and then the pain would stop.

He marched towards the window, picking up another chair along the way, and heaved it at its center. A large crack dashed its surface, like a spider's web. He picked the chair up from the floor and gave another swing. Two did the trick.

He stood on the balcony, hands gripping the jagged frame, his toes over the ledge.

Maybe I could fly away from this place, he thought to himself.

Sarah stood and stared at the red patch on the ground. After a while, the cameras had stopped flashing and had left the scene. The ambulance had departed. The cleanup crew had done a decent enough job, but a small red patch remained, marked across a crack in the sidewalk, left to harden and brown so that the ants might carry it away.

Allen Wyckoff was gone.

"Anything more we can do for you, ma'am?"

"No, thank you," she spoke without looking towards the police officers. "Just thinking, that's all." He nodded, and after providing her some official contact information, departed. She pocketed the business card and made her way inside of building seventeen.

Allen Wyckoff was gone. She'd known him since freshman year. They'd shared moments of struggle and togetherness. From sharing notes in first calculus to graduation. And now he was taken from her.

She walked through the dark corridors, past the empty work desks, past the empty room with the broken window and the caution tape stretched across the door and made her way to the storage room. She fumbled with the light for a moment before walking over to the far shelves. She sifted through boxes of flash memory cards and data crystals, miscellaneous computer hardware, and other assorted rubbish before she found what she wanted.

A single inconspicuous silver box.

She produced a key from her pocket and opened it, gazing upon the Koleshkova scanner.

It was an entirely unremarkable device. A headset with some wires, and three small plastic boxes that held the necessary electronic components. A single thick cable ran down from one side, with a port on its end. That's all it took.

Sarah felt tears welling up. This device. This wretched device had taken from here. This horrible thing had stolen somebody away from here, taken a piece of her own life.

Her hands tensed up. It'd be so easy to do away with it, she thought. Take it home with her in the darkness of the night. Bring a welder to it, burn it, melt it down to unrecognizable slag. If she was careful, nobody would notice it was gone for months, maybe. At that point, nobody could point a finger at her any sooner than they could point towards anybody else in the hundred-person team.

Sarah's hands trembled. She took a deep breath, and they calmed along with her.

Dr. Wilson lowered the device back into the foam padding within its box and closed the lid. She locked it, put the key back into her pocket, and placed the case back onto the shelf. She put her hands in her pockets, turned around, and walked out of the storage room.

Dr. Wilson prided herself in being a rational, analytical person. Indeed, she felt ashamed. The Koleshkova scanner wasn't to blame – it was only a medium for the problem. If she destroyed it, it could and would be replaced. Already, she had little doubt that people worldwide were working hard on recreating it.

She'd need to be responsible, she thought to herself as she made her way out of the laboratory. Promote some way that would prevent this from happening again. That would prohibit anyone from being taken away like this. A safeguard from tragedy.

An artificial intelligence made from fundamental principles. Something born from the machine.

Something that would feel at home in itself.

The ideas were already churning through her mind as she stepped into an auto and punched in her home address.

Chapter 8

The doorbell rang. On time with precision. It was bothersome, for some reason.

A6 walked to the door and opened it. Before it stood a somewhat portly looking gentleman. He was sporting a small pair of glasses, neatly trimmed hair, and a short, full-faced beard. Every hair on him was some variant of salt-and-pepper gray. He held a clipboard in hand, scrawled with messy chicken scratch. He smiled as he spoke.

"Morning there. My name's Randall. I'm with the I.E.B. Ambassador Program. Mind if I get your name? Just to make sure I'm at the right place for today's appointment?"

A6 bared its teeth into a toothy expression that only vaguely resembled a smile. With eyebrows clicked into a lowered position, it tilted its head to the side and began rattling off its serial code in monotone.

"A6R4P1832795." Upon finishing, it thereby promptly began waiting for the annoying human at the door to either say it wrong or to dodge the response entirely.

Randall's smile curled into a knowing smirk. "Right! That's what I thought. Lovely meeting you then, A6R4P1832795," he recited, never once breaking eye contact. "Do you mind terribly if I come in?"

In that exact moment, A6 wanted nothing more in the entire world than to slam the door into his wholesome, jolly face. Just the very thought of a broken nose and shattered pair of glasses adorning contented its very metallic soul.

But it was also legal obligations. And as unfortunate as it was, this bastard, in particular, was the one that had power over him.

"Enter," it spoke in as flat a tone as possible, before backing out of the doorway, allowing the unwelcome guest into its dwelling. Randall took a few steps in and admired the room for a bit. His eyes fell at last upon the furniture. "Do you mind terribly if I sit on the couch?"

"Sit." To its dismay, he did, and A6 resigned itself to sitting opposite of him, hands in its lap.

Randall took a moment to sift through the papers on his clipboard while A6 dedicated its time to glaring at him. Finally, he spoke. "Now, if I've done my homework correctly, you're presently on service orders for assaulting a human pedestrian on the streets of Grand, along the coastal region, Sunday before last. That correct?"

"That depends rather heavily on what you mean by 'assault'."

Randall reorganized his papers and set his clipboard off to the side. "Well then. It'd only be fair for me to listen to your side of the story then, wouldn't it? Not just what the court told me about you. Go on, what's your perspective?"

Fair.

The word lingered in the air, stubborn, unwilling to depart. And it angered A6 more than anything else that this invader had dared to say or do up until this point. What did he know about fairness? What right did he have to enter its domicile and use that word like that as though he had any idea of what it meant?

"I was heading East on Grand Ave, on the way towards my credit union to make a deposit. Along the way, a stranger shoved me and spat a racial slur at my direction. When he came at me again, I shoved him away from me. He tripped backward on a curb and hit the back of his skull against the pavement. He was briefly hospitalized and discharged later the same day with no permanent injuries to show for it."

Randall had begun idly stroking his beard. In response, A6 seethed. It logged a reminder in its system to clean up the loose hairs and dead skin cells after he'd inevitably leave behind.

"Well, I mean, it's no wonder you're upset. I imagine that, had the roles been reversed, the human would have gotten off rather lightly. And that the court is rather unwilling to so much as humor your perspective is disheartening. I understand how you feel, and-"

And that was too much.

A6 leaned forward and slammed its fists down on the coffee table that sat between them. It shot up and jabbed a mechanical finger at Randall's mug, and – breaking its otherwise monotone speech – began screaming at him.

"Oh, you think you know how it feels, fucker? You think you can say with a straight face that you know anything about how it feels to be born into ostracism. Get off your high-fucking-horse, old man, about your self-purported wisdom concerning exactly how I ought to change my ways. Either that or get the fuck out of my dwelling."

It was at this moment that Randall did something A6 never expected.

Randall kept a calm expression and squeezed his right bicep using only his index and thumb from his left hand, popping his arm off.

"Catch," he said, tossing his dismembered limb out towards A6 with a soft underhand.

A6 held out both arms and caught the appendage. Even if the confusion it experienced in its processor was resolved in less than a fraction of a second, it still made the duration of time that the illusion lasted no less uncomfortable. As it looked it over, it took note of all the little details that made its formulation complete.

"It's a prosthetic."

"I was born without my right arm," spoke Randall, through a somber expression. "This was back during the last few years of the 20th century when crude metal hooks and rubbery plastics were still commonly used in prosthesis. The technology needed to achieve greater realism existed, of course, but it was still prohibitively expensive, and my parents were only just getting by around that point."

Randall got up from his spot on the couch, walked over to A6 to looked it over. "I'm not entirely surprised you didn't notice it wasn't real at first glance. I've only ever had it pointed out by others a few times since I got it – usually by the occasional odd duck who decided they wanted thermal vision. I've even donated the hairs from my other arm, just to keep it as close to real as possible. I guess I still have a hard time accepting myself.

"But even today, with some of the better technology, it's never quite the same as my other arm. The sensation at the fingertips is rather extreme: always telling me that something's either much hotter or much colder than my other hand does. Outside of the fingers, it's quite numb everywhere else. And even if it's nimbler, and my reflexes are faster with it, I always find myself requiring the support of my other hand to lift even moderately heavy objects. That's just the tradeoff."

Randall plucked up the limb from out of A6's hands and plugged it back into his stump. He calibrated it for a little bit, wiggling his fingers a bit, and let it fall to rest at his side again. "Growing up, a lot of people around me had some sort of assumption that I was disabled, somehow. I never much liked the term. I always thought that I could be capable of doing everything that other people could do, even if I ultimately had to do it differently. Other people expressed their sorrow for me. I never much understood that, either. I had never grown up with a proper right arm: I never felt like there was anything lost. For me, it was just always that way. It was just normal."

A6 began to realize that it had been staring into the palms of its own hands in silence for a little bit too long. It turned its head up and looked into Randall's eyes. Randall gave an expression halfway between a smile and a grimace, before continuing.

"I think a lot of people think you have to be just like them to be considered normal, or functional, or even a person worthy of their time and attention. But growing up the way I did, I never really got that. Straight from the start, I guess I just came to acknowledge my differences, and with them, the differences of others. Just because somebody's different than you don't mean that they deserve any less respect or decent treatment as a person."

An odd silence hovered over the room. Finally, Randall sighed and adjusted his glasses. "Listen, A6R4P183-"

"A6," it said, fighting an instinct to hold its right arm in its left hand. "If it's any more comfortable for you, or otherwise easier to remember, you may refer to me as A6."

Randall's smile grew just a fraction. "Look, A6. You're right. I can't understand how you feel. Nobody can. Nobody but you. But I might have had a few experiences similar to yours, whether I wanted them or not. And maybe it's part of the reason I chose to do the work I do now. I figured that, regardless of the darker motivations of more than a few chapters of the I.E.B. Ambassador Program, at the very least, I can try to make a difference with the utmost sincerity. I don't just have to be your effective probation officer. And I do truly mean it when I say that I believe that just because we're different doesn't mean we're not both deserving of being treated the way people ought to be treated."

Randall picked up his clipboard and headed towards the door. With his hand on the doorknob, he stopped and turning around. "Today was just meant to be a check-in. However, I won't force you to speak with me when I'm obligated to come over again next week. I believe these sorts of interactions can't be forced. If you don't feel like talking, just say so at the door, and I'll sign the document saying that we went over everything."

"Alright."

"Is there anything else I ought to say?"

"No, thank you." Said A6.

Randall nodded. "Take care of yourself, A6."

Then he closed the door behind him, and just like that, he was gone.

A6 resolved to plug itself in for the night. It was still early in the evening, but for some reason, it felt more emotionally exhausted than it had felt in months.

Chapter 9

President Fischer tossed back the last few sips of her coffee in a quick gulp before turning to her next cup. The morning became less insufferable this way, but it didn't seem to slow the rate that her hairs grayed.

"Right. Let's make this quick. Give me a brief update about the midterm state election in Colorado. I'll be honest, it hasn't exactly been a primary concern for me. I'm not ashamed to confess my ignorance, so please, start from the beginning."

Derek tapped his papers on the table to straighten them out. "Well, things have been tricky there, to say the least. What started as an experiment in democracy has turned into a complicated issue ultimately resulting in statewide protest."

"And the background behind it all?"

"Well, see, it's been about seven years since the I.E.B. leak brought upon the world via the Viral Brigade, and with it, seven years since we saw the first I.E.B.s to be birthed into the world outside the confines of government-funded institutions. With that in mind, professional researchers and neuroscientists have come up with varying interpretations, but most seem to agree that most artificial intelligences reach a state of 'maturity' within five years."

Fischer raised an eyebrow. "Most."

"Well, sure. I.E.B.s are rather diverse and are already numbered in the thousands. There exist forms that, though sentient, contain subhuman intelligence, and never mature past their original point of formation. And there are identical neuro-emulation scans of children's brains who reach maturity the same rate that a human might. It's impossible to put all I.E.B.s under the same classifiers when it concerns much of anything outside of their fundamental requirements."

"And I take it this was part of the issue that struck Colorado."

"It's certainly a contributing factor. The state decided that to provide a temporary remedy for the issue, they'd focus on implementing professional maturity tests to ensure that I.E.B.s who were already declared citizens and were looking to vote either met or exceeded the minimum maturity of the average human adult."

Fischer couldn't help but shake her head. "If history's any indicator, voter tests have proven to be a terrible solution. Legally, I imagine that conflicts with the 14th. How horrible is the outrage so far?"

"It's depended on the county, but you're otherwise right to be pessimistic, ma'am. Some of the more conservative counties hired unreliable testers and ruled out virtually all applying I.E.B.s. However, in the more progressive counties that were more densely populated with I.E.B.s, applicability was nearly universal. Accounts reported a neuro-emulation copy of an underage boy successfully applying to vote on his base human's behalf. So far, conservatives have been using that as a scare tactic."

"Explain?"

"Their argument is if I.E.B.s are permitted the right to vote, that there would be nothing stopping a single organization from forming several thousand neuro-emulations of an individual that was tasked with voting for one party or measure, jeopardizing the election. The entire system of power would be handed over to whoever could afford the most processors to run each copy."

"I dunno," spoke Fischer with a dry tone. "Doesn't sound too different from our current system."

It caused a few scattered guffaws about the conference room.

She changed her focus. "How much has I.E.B. participation affected turnout?"

"It's estimated that of all the I.E.B.s in the state, 70% were considered eligible by the standards in their respective counties. Of those, 71% were successful in their endeavor.

Fischer mulled it over. "That's a higher turnout rate than most human voters."

"That it is. In fact, it about matches the turnout rate of human voters in Colorado just over one century ago."

"And the results of the election?"

"Not a big surprise. Progressive candidates and propositions won out. Conservatives are upset and are calling for a proper investigation on the cases of unqualified voters to determine whether or not the number would change any of the outcomes."

Fischer turned to Alex. "Alex, I want you to see if you can't write me up a bill, with the consultation of a few hand-picked professionals in the field. I've heard good things from Doctor Sarah Wilson. She was head of the department that made Katie early in the program, right?"

"Yes, that's right," said Alex, still stiffened from when Fischer had called out his name.

"I want a bill written up and on standby. One that addresses I.E.B.s and their statutes for voting. Original intelligence and synthetic intelligence will be held to a five-year age requirement since their date of creation. Neuro-emulations will be eligible to vote only when their age, together with the age of their base human at the time of the scan exceeds eighteen."

"Mrs. President, wouldn't this pose a risk of furthering the problem of duplicate votes?"

"Historically, duplicate votes have been a minuscule portion of all voting discrepancies – very few people are ever bothered enough to want to do so when there are other, simpler methods of committing voter fraud. In fact, last I checked, the number of cases was found to be in the single digits last year, compared to the thousands of votes cast by a deceased voter. Already, making and registering a neuro-emulation has been discouraged through the bureaucratic process since A-Prime's demise. I think we have far more pressing matters to worry about."

"And when will this bill be passed unto congress?"

"It won't be."

Alex and Derek were only a few of the sets of eyes that stared at her in silence.

"….sorry?"

"For now, I.E.B.s aren't a significant portion of the voter population. Beyond that, they don't have personal needs on par with human needs. They aren't as affected by the aftermath of the economic collapse my administration inherited. They don't have mouths to feed. They don't have healthcare costs to tend to. The entirety of what they require consists of electricity and maintenance, and nothing more. I cater to human voters, with needs much more pressing. Sure, if I can get more voters – human or machine – on my side for re-election, great. But until more I.E.B.s start pushing for that particular right, the bill will be shelved for when it can be used as a point of policy during debates. Until then, it'll be too much of a hell trying to get passed through ravenous opponents in Senate to even consider getting it looked over."

An uncomfortable air filled the room. Derek finally broke the silence. "Mrs. President, a concern."

"Speak."

"Well…. this is all fine and well for the short term, but… What do you suppose will happen when an I.E.B. tries to run for an official office? Or even your position?"

Fischer finished her coffee and pursed her lips. "It wouldn't ever happen. Conservative opponents wouldn't ever let it occur. If not in registration, then in competition. They'd be voted off the ballot the moment somebody saw a serial number in place of a name next to the checkbox."

"Well, sure, that might be the case now. But it's still quite a bit more plausible to imagine a singular android running for office than it is for a coherent system that permits all of them to register to vote within strict guidelines."

Fischer contemplated the matter. It felt uncomfortable to acknowledge that she hadn't considered the possibility on her own before. Just another reminder to be grateful for her cabinet. With all the times they'd pointed out flaws or offered suggestions, she knew she wouldn't be here without them. "I'll have to think it over. For now, we're over time. Get to work on that bill, Alex."

Chapter 10

Project Log Day 431

As per Dr. Wilson's demands, Katie was to spend as little time activated and without a physical body as possible. Thankfully, it had been managed, and Katie had been performing exceptionally well so far. Her mental capacities had proven strong, and her processor had matched every requirement for sentience the team had defined a few months back.

Tests with her body's interaction with the physical world were a little rockier, however. Walking proved to be especially difficult, and it required almost all of Katie's concentration to perform a smooth stride. Object detection was fast, but it still took a few seconds for her to identify the face of a colleague. The task of writing was perhaps the most challenging. Katie had picked up the bad habit of writing with stiff fingers and a pivoting wrist. Sarah did her best to humor Katie's practice, but tried to redirect the behavior to a level of dexterity comparable to a human.

After a few months of testing, the day finally came to hold a conference between the members of the project and the leading university chief staff concerning the need for Katie's further development and maturity.

The meeting began. Doctor Wilson stood up and made her opening with very little hesitation.

"Good afternoon, ladies and gentlemen. My name is Doctor Sarah Wilson. I speak on behalf of the university's Intelligent Electronic Brain subdivision. Since Allen's passing last year, the public eye has been incredibly critical about the possibility and application of sentient artificial intelligence. Steps with Katie have proven valuable, but donors remain hesitant – especially with the lack of public exposure we've made of her."

There was no idle banter. The conference room had been silent until her remarks. The university president, Adam Henry, gently leaned forward and spoke.

"Doctor Wilson, I think I speak for everybody in the room when I say that we're all deeply upset over the passing of Allen. Our institution has been marked, rendered synonymous with the incident. However, we all recognize the need to push forward: during the experiments undertaken involving brain mapping and emulation, we received more public funding than we had ever received for a single individual project before. The people before you are entirely convinced, Dr. Wilson. You need not speak any further on that subject. If anything at all, we want to know what solution your team will propose to reestablish funding."

Dr. Wilson didn't miss a beat. "We want to try to develop Katie to the point where she could resemble an adult human female in everyday interactions. We believe that once she's attained enough knowledge and social experience, she'll resemble a proper ambassador for our campus. Institutions around the globe have already begun creating fundamental A.I.'s, based off of the shared public development. But by proving to the world that such an intelligence can inhabit a physical body, one that can interact with the world in a manner similar to how you or I might, we'll stand out to investors with our lead in the A.I. development race."

President Henry simply folded his hands and held his eyebrows up. "And what sort of experience will she require? What kind of education would you want her to be exposed to?"

Sarah gripped the lectern with both hands. "We don't want to expose her to the student population quite just yet – we think that it would have the potential to overwhelm her with unneeded attention at best and threaten her livelihood at worst. As a group, we've come up with a proposition: our team would like to grant Katie access to the library after closing hours."

After the discussion was finalized, the team had agreed to permit Katie – along with one other faculty member at a time – to have unrestricted access to the library after midnight on Mondays, Tuesdays, and Wednesdays. The question arose concerning the possibility of Katie using online resources, so as to secure the safety of her physical body. The idea was rebutted with the threat of online invasion to Katie's systems: her progress was too valuable to risk it for now.

A compromise was established for Thursdays onward. If Katie demonstrated a positive reaction to the daily routine and wanted to make it a regular habit, then she'd need to attend the library during regular hours. This would hopefully, according to Brian, help establish a sense of normality among new people. While controversy boiled through the group over the details, most agreed that it would be a worthwhile step to take, provided she was accompanied by project members, and only attended during quieter hours. In turn, Dr. Wilson suggested that she'd consult Katie about the matter when the time came.

Monday came.

At eleven o' clock at night, Sarah walked into the primary testing room, where Katie was working with Robert on memory management tests. Sarah watched her for a few minutes, taking note of her performance and focus.

Upon completion of the latest trial, Brian looked up and nodded to her. Sarah smiled, stepped forward, and spoke.

"Hi, Katie."

Katie turned and looked up at Sarah. A few seconds ticked by. "Good evening, Sarah! How do you think I'm doing so far?"

"I think you're doing wonderfully, Katie. In fact, you've exceeded all of our expected parameters."

Katie nodded, and quickly went back to facing Robert to continue testing. When he didn't mirror her motions, she furrowed her brow. Without looking back up to Sarah, she spoke. "I want to continue practicing. I feel like I haven't done well enough on it yet. I find it comforting. May we resume?"

Sarah pulled in a chair and sat down next to Katie. "I'd like to try something new with you today, Katie. I'd like to establish a new routine. It'll be another sort of a test. How would you like to visit the campus library with me?"

Katie turned to look at Sarah again with a somewhat blank face. "The campus library. Am I going to leave the testing center?"

"That's correct, Katie."

Katie looked away and thought for several seconds. Robert and Sarah waited for her to respond. Time had proven that Katie was very good at worrying about things, and she didn't often like being interrupted when she was busy with it. Finally, Katie got up and walked to the corner of the room, staring at the wall with hands held closed at her sides. After a few more minutes, she turned to face Sarah again.

"It sounds very interesting. And I want another routine. However, I have my concerns. I'm afraid. Will there be other people there? How will I get there?"

"The library is closed right now, Katie. But the president gave me a key, and said you'd be able to have the library to yourself from twelve to three in the morning, Monday through Wednesday, so long as somebody on the team was there with you." Sarah considered her words with precision – Katie had developed the habit of making literal interpretations.

"I'd like to attend, then. How will I get there?"

Sarah closed the massive library doors behind them. With an audible thud that echoed through the depths of the halls, Katie's night at the library had officially begun. She pocketed the keys and readjusted her grip on the briefcase containing spare batteries for Katie, along with her personal laptop.

The halls were quiet enough that Katie's otherwise inaudible servos emitted a sort whirring sound with every little movement she made. She walked through the corridors, taking in every image with fervent curiosity.

"Feel free to go wherever you'd like, Katie. Every book is entirely at your access. Just try not to damage anything, and to put everything back where you found it. I'll be close behind you."

Katie processed the suggestion for a moment, then chose a random direction, striding down the corridors with a sense of determination. Sarah struggled somewhat to keep up; it was clear that, despite Katie's fairly blank expression, her actions expressed excitement.

After a few corridors, two staircases, and a short walk to one shelf in particular, Katie began drawing books. She'd scan the cover, open a few pages, decipher the words. She began setting some books aside while shelving others in their original place. Content that she was making comprehensive judgments, Sarah found a quiet spot on the floor near an outlet to sit down. She plugged in her laptop and started remotely monitoring Katie's mental reactions. Squiggles and lines indicating her faux-vitals crossed the window. Satisfied that the program was recording every thought, Sarah eased back and opened her own work in a new tab.

"Sarah, can you tell me more about what this means?"

Sarah woke up with a start. Her eyes were first greeted with the laptop's screen, and its detailed illustration of the large spikes of activity in Katie's mind. Katie was looming above her and holding a small book in her hands. Behind her on the floor sat several, perfectly leveled stacks of books removed from the shelf.

Sarah adjusted her glasses and reached out for the book. Katie placed the book on her hand, and Sarah looked it over. She read the title out loud.

"I, Robot - Isaac Asimov"

Oh no.

At that very moment, Sarah felt as though she were explaining the meaning of a swear word to a child – the very first child the world had ever seen. She suddenly became quite aware of how tall Katie stood above her – the long shadow that she cast, and the cold, metallic glint in her eye as she gazed down upon her.

"Well, Katie…. just about a century ago, there were authors who were fascinated by robotics. They didn't have the technology to understand or predict the implications of the matter."

Katie continued her intent stare but nodded with a sense of comprehension. "I'm bad at making predictions too."

Sarah gave a cool exhale through pursed lips. "I take it you read the part about the universal laws of robotics, then. Right?"

Katie recited:

"First: A robot may not injure a human being or, through inaction, allow a human being to come to harm. Second: A robot must obey the orders given it by human beings except where such orders would conflict with the First Law. Third: A robot must protect its own existence as long as such protection does not conflict with the First or Second Laws."

Sarah nodded. "That's correct, yes."

Katie's face twisted into something of a hurt expression. Sarah's mind quickly feared for the worst; it wasn't very often that Katie expressed herself so vividly, and it usually meant something horrible was about to happen. She gently rose to her feet, doing everything in her power to retain the calm atmosphere.

"I don't like it, Sarah. I see conflict when I read them."

Sarah took meticulous care in her choice of words. "What conflict do you see?"

"What would happen if a human tried to hurt me? Or kill me? I'm alive, just like they are. If I tried to kill a human, wouldn't that be just as bad?"

"Well, yes, according to those rules, but-"

"So why did he make it a rule that humans would be allowed to hurt robots while making it impossible for robots to defend themselves?"

"Well, Katie, I don-"

"Is that really what humans think of beings like me?"

Sarah sighed folded the book under her arm. "Katie, a century ago, writers didn't think very hard about the possibility of I.E.B.s or androids like you. At the time, they mostly just considered the possibilities of robots acting either as servants, or otherwise as a danger to humankind. They were confused; they wanted to ask questions, to get people thinking and talking about these topics so that they might be able to understand them a little bit better."

"You think that's the case."

"Oh, I know that's the case," said Sarah, placing her free hand on Katie's shoulder. "I'd wager that humans are very animal-like in our thinking. When we look at something like a tiger, we often find ourselves weighing our possible interactions with it. Deciding whether we ought to be afraid of it or take advantage of it. Whether we should treat it as more as a pet or a threat. I don't think it crosses our minds that an animal like a tiger might simply not want to have anything to do with us – that a tiger can simply be, never mind the presence of the human. We just don't consider it much. Not immediately, anyway."

Katie's expression softened, and her eyes lowered. "I think I can accept that perspective, Sarah. Even if I don't like it much."

"I don't think these rules should ever have to apply to somebody like you, Katie. You're more than metal and plastic, just as I'm more than a chunk of carbon and water and salt. You're alive. I think you should be beholden to the same moral rules that govern all thinking beings, whatever we decide they might be."

Dr. Wilson walked straight over to the nearest shelf and placed the book back where it belonged.

"Let me know if you have any more questions. Alright?"

"Yes." And without hesitation, Katie returned to the shelves to resume her task of sorting through the books and establish her piles.

Likewise, Sarah wasted no time returning to her laptop to catch up on the work she missed while she'd nodded off. She figured that they'd both be here for at least a few more hours.

But as she watched Katie scanning the pages from the corner of her vision, her mind couldn't seem to leave the conversation they'd just had.

Chapter 11

Randall straightened his tie, cleared his throat, and knocked.

"Hello? Who's there?" spoke a squeaky voice from the other side of the door.

"That'd be Randall Anderson. I'm the I.E.B. Ambassador scheduled for today's meeting with a Sally. Is this the right place?"

A short class five android peeked through the door with a smile. Well, maybe a perfect class five was being generous. She was just skirting the edge of human likeness: with pale white skin, neon pink eyes, long pink hair done in pigtails, and a summer dress that fit just a little bit too flat and tight, she would have stuck out as unusual in any crowd. Even among those who modified their bodies to extremes, everything about her just seemed too deliberate and tidy to be human.

Her eyes clicked up and down, scanning Randall's appearance. Satisfied with what she saw, she smiled, curtsied politely, and opened the door with an inviting motion of the hand. "Indeed, you are! Please, do come in!"

Randall nodded, folded his clipboard back under his arm, and strode into the house. Looking around, he noted the significant depth of the place. Her home had a sort of a craftsman aesthetic to it. Back when he was a prohibition officer, few homes were as neat as hers.

The android girl closed the door behind him. "Tell me, can I get you anything. Do you prefer coffee? Tea?"

Randall paused. "I suppose that largely depends on the situation. And the quality of the tea. Are you a stickler? Do we have loose leaf English breakfast?"

"As a matter of fact, we do! Just a moment!" And with that, she disappeared down the hallway to the right.

A voice to his left called out, "The kitchen's just this way!"

Puzzled, Randall followed the voice into the kitchen to find the same android girl operating a kettle at the stove top. Steam was already pouring out from it. She turned to Randall with a smile that betrayed just a hint of mischief. "If you wouldn't mind helping out, you could get some teacups from the glass cupboard in the dining room." She nodded towards the walkway opposite of him.

Apprehensive as he was, he wasn't yet unwilling to humor her. Randall walked across the kitchen and into the dining room. There, sitting at the table next to the glass cupboard, sat yet again the same exact android girl, sewing together a dress – a dress identical to the one she was wearing. Randall stopped, opened his mouth, but instead decided to take a trail not so oft-trodden.

"Remind me: exactly why is it that you have so many teacups when most I.E.B.'s don't consume liquid outside of servo lubricant or hydraulic fluid?"

"Or, I certainly don't drink tea myself, if that's what you're getting after. But I do enjoy the aroma it produces. Sometimes, I just let a kettle full of tea out to simmer until the entire house of filled with the warm scent. Besides that, they provide a wonderful aesthetic, and they make a good offering to guests. And they're just so much fun to collect! It is a nice collection, isn't it?"

Without waiting for an answer, the android girl made one last securing stitch in the fabric, stood up, folded the garment, and disappeared through the hallway to Randall's left. No sooner had she departed when the same exact android appeared at Randall's right, holding a tray with a kettle, a bowl of sugar, some milk, and a few pastries. She set it down at the table and smiled. Randall remembered his reason for entering, and hastily procured two of the nicer teacups and a pair of saucers from the cupboard before taking a seat beside her. She nodded with approval.

"A man of taste, I see – those happen to be two of my favorite cups."

He raised an eyebrow. "I'm surprised that you don't consider all of them to be your favorites."

Sally only looked away and smiled a little, saying nothing.

Randall couldn't suppress a smirk. "Forgive me for asking. But I did come here to speak with Sally. Exactly whom should I be addressing?"

Three identical androids poked their heads through the entryways and together in a perfect quartet unison, spoke: "That'd be me!"

It was exceedingly uncommon, but it wasn't unheard of for an I.E.B. to control multiple bodies simultaneously. The processing power and electrical requirements were multiplied and often made it prohibitively expensive. But for those who could afford it, some preferred the extra eyes and hands, or even the ability to mitigate opportunity loss. Randall himself regularly wished for the ability to be in two places at once. Or even the ability to allow one version of himself to sleep while another stayed up at night, working over the endless stack of incident paperwork.

"Very well then," he said, as he reconsidered his phrasing. "Which 'Sally' is the one that contains her processor?"

Three of the Sallys by the entryways quietly slunk away, while the tea kettle Sally sat down at the table, a dim red LED glow crossing her cheeks.

He smiled with just a bit of satisfaction, satisfied that he'd caught up with her mischief. I.E.B.'s, Randall reflected, couldn't exist on multiple processors simultaneously. Not for long, anyway. Attempts had been made, but the philosophy got complex. If a single consciousness occupied two separate processors at the same time, problems emerged when a disconnect between the two happened. Depending on the structure, the I.E.B. would either be killed instantly, or split into two separate consciousnesses, each one marked unique, based off their own personal experiences. Much like identical twins might behave differently, based on each of their personal experiences in life.

As she poured his cup of tea, another thought crossed his mind. "While we're on that topic, there wouldn't happen to be anybody else living upstairs with you, would there?" He asked, tapping the side of his head.

"Oh, goodness no. Call me selfish, but it's always just been me living in my own processor."

There'd been occasions where multiple I.E.B.'s could and have existed on a single processor. Erroneously nicknamed "multiple personality units," they often faced similar problems as those with a split consciousness: it's entirely impossible to transfer a persisting state of consciousness from one location to the next, short of copying it. At this point, the old consciousness hasn't been moved, only duplicated to a new location separate from its fellow occupants, which marks it, again, as its own unique individual.

Of the few I.E.B.'s who adopted multiple bodies, virtually all of them preferred to choose a single dedicated body as the carrier of the processor. This made for a system of multiple bodies controlled with one brain, with each of the other units housing a radio receiver in place of a processor. It wasn't without its flaws, of course: a connection loss, for example, could cause any of the body copies to simply slump over right where they were. Sally appeared to adopt this model: though each of the bodies appeared identical, it was only the Sally that sat before him, teacup in hand, that by itself housed everything that made Sally Sally.

Randall took another sip from his tea, before returning his cup to its saucer. "Now then, Sally. I'm here today because of an incident in your file. I have the paperwork with me, but I find that it's never the whole picture. Would you mind terribly if I got your side of the story?"

Sally stiffened up rather considerably. "Well, I really don't think that there's very much worth saying. I think it boils down to a mere misunderstanding."

Randall referred to his clipboard. "According to the accusations of the shop owner, you were exhibiting suspicious behavior on store property, which led her to suspect fraud or shoplifting."

The sound of something delicate shattering against the floor echoed down the hallway to his left. It was followed by the sound of a door slamming somewhere upstairs.

"She said it was suspicious enough of shoplifting. Is that what she said."

Randall scanned his clipboard again. "Those were her words, yes."

"Okay. So I bring three separate items to the cashier in three separate pairs of hands and ask questions about each one with just a little bit too much enthusiasm. And somehow, this somehow justifies an officer called to the scene and a mandated meeting with an ambassador. Somebody to come to listen to the 'problem' and to 'fix' me."

As Randall studied her expression, he found himself with the inexplicable suspicion that there happened to be another Sally lurking behind him somewhere down the hall. Randall reached for the cream and sugar, added a small dose of each to his tea, and took a small sip.

"Don't be so quick to think that I haven't heard of this sort of occasions before, Sally – from both human and I.E.B. interactions. We tend to be very apprehensive about anything that's different from ourselves. And we look to justify our act of ostracizing anything that's even just a little bit out of place. Watch me try to get through the airport security while wearing a pair of pants on my head. Even if I hadn't done anything illegal, I can't imagine that'd go over very well."

Sally's previously hostile expression was marred with puzzlement. Randall took advantage of the silence by finishing his tea before he continued.

"The fact of the matter is, Sally, that I'm not here to 'fix' you, because you're not broken – nobody should ever have to 'fix' you. And if anybody has the audacity to try, you shouldn't have to put up with it. I'm only here to fix a broken relationship between two different cultures, starting with people on either side, one person at a time. That's what my job is."

Sally relaxed somewhat but otherwise remained still. "Right... Sorry about lashing out."

"Quite alright. Now, do you mind terribly if we continue?"

"I suppose."

He referred to his clipboard again. "The file I was handed mentioned the store and the name of the owner, but they didn't make mention of the finer details. If you don't mind me asking, just what items of personal curiosity were so fascinating that it called you to the cashier so much?"

Sally perked up somewhat. "Teacups!"

Randall couldn't help but smile. "Of course. You know, that was some very nice tea. Hard to find quality like this with all the embargos."

"Thank you very much. Care for some more? Should I give you the name of the supplier?"

"Maybe. Before I leave, anyway." Randall leaned back in his seat and mulled over the details of his empty teacup. Everything was going to end up just fine between them. That much he was certain about.

Chapter 12

"Next in line, please."

The tall man with the slight stubble and short hair raised his hand and cleared his throat, before stepping forward. He folded his overcoat, placed it the bin next to his shoes for the x-ray machine, and walked through the metal detector.

Fischer took a sharp swig from her mug as she watched the man on the projector screen pass through the plastic arch. There was a shrill beeping sound, and the agent opposite of him raised a blue latex hand. The man stepped back, and a separate agent approached from the side with a personal metal detector wand. Waving it across his body, the discrepancy was discovered: the stubble man removed his belt, placed it in the adjacent bin, and continued through. No further alarm.

"Sir, if you wouldn't mind stepping this way for a bit?"

The stubble man stopped mid-stride with eyebrows raised, but nodded and complied, despite visible indication of his inconvenienced status. The agent motioned to a chair, and he took a seat, hands placed folded on his lap. The agent drew forward a thin silver briefcase and opened it, revealing a variety of instruments.

A small circular aluminum sticker was produced and peeled. A swab of antiseptic later, and it was placed on the man's neck. The monitor on the briefcase released a series of cheerful tones — pulse and breathing looked good. The agent nodded and gave the man a quick tap on the kneecap with a pocked-sized reflex hammer. A sharp jump of the leg. The agent offered a short metal straw. The man wrapped his lips around it and exhaled. Another cheerful beep.

"Right. All looks fine and well. Thank you for your time, have a nice flight?"

The stubbled man stood up and smiled. "Sure thing. You have a nice day."

The man went to retrieve his overcoat and shoes, making haste to put them on and grab his luggage, so as not to inconvenience the growing crowd behind him.

He passed through the hallways, rounded the corner, and made his way past a pair of airport security officers.

In one inhuman and calculated series of motions, he elbowed one officer in the face, dropped to the floor alongside him, swiped his firearm, and disposed of the adjacent officer with a single shot. Onlookers screamed as he pulled the MP5 submachine gun from the late officer's hip and made his way towards the nearest crowd.

"Down on the ground. Hands on your heads, and heads down. Hurry up!"

As he made his way down the halls, the man seized the wrist of a screaming girl — no older than six years old — and hoisted her body up to his chest level, alarms blared throughout the airport. A pair of officers rounded the corner. The man's arm whipped upwards and connected one shot to each of the officer's foreheads as he made his way to the nearest terminal. Shouts filled the air. He pointed the weapon to the ticketing agent and started barking orders.

"You! I want this entire airplane cleared of passengers. I want them lined up here in single file, poi-"

A single shot rang through the air, and the terrorist fell to his knees, the girl in his arm running from his clutches. As his face contacted the floor, the camera zoomed in on the digital readout behind his eyes. Military officers gathered around, each proudly wearing the United States flag on their uniforms, weapons trained on the limp android body. The screen went blurry, text emerging from its center.

"A class six android could emerge at any moment. Do your part to keep our nation safe from the I.E.B. threat? Vote "NO" on proposition 63 to reduce our defense budget."

The screen went black, and the lights in the room turned on again. All eyes turned to Fischer. She set down her coffee, steepled her fingers, and took her time in selecting the most appropriate words.

"Well. That was stupid. Really, really goddamn stupid. Can't wait to see the national reaction to that one."

Derek stood with mouth slightly agape, his face marked with concern. In his silence, Alex spoke up.

"Mrs. President, the cabinet has come together in unanimous agreement: we're concerned about the possible effect this attack ad could have on our chances of passing prop 63, should it gain traction upon its release tomorrow afternoon. We've already assembled a team of lawyers to strike it down as a violation of hate speech laws..."

"Won't do any good," said Fischer, taking another sip from her mug. "Trying to hide it from the public eye will only mark it as forbidden fruit and make it all the more appealing while labeling our administration as censors of public discourse. If we sit back and let it happen, we won't risk jeopardizing our moral high ground."

Derek finally found himself composed enough to chime in. "But surely, Mrs. President, you must agree that this level of propaganda is a legitimate threat to our administrative goals."

"Even if it is, nothing good can come from trying to derail it. As it stands, Callahan's campaign for election strikes me as being fundamentally flawed in its approach. Each new work of propaganda his organization churns out does little more than appeal to those who are already fearfully dedicated to him, while further alienating undecided voters. I believe that the worst we could do at this point would be to stop him from shooting himself in the foot. Besides that, this particular attack ad carries a number of fatal flaws."

"Care to clarify?"

As Fischer spoke, she stood up and walked over to the nearby coffee machine to pour herself another cup.

"As you're aware, Alex, I.E.B. bodies are unofficially ordered by class, by means of human likeness, on a scale from zero to five. Class zero bodies are rather immobile machines, usually reducible to a single processor, though as a general rule, they're certainly not lacking human levels of intelligence — the International Space Station's latest incarnation, 'Alexander' is an excellent example of that — while class five androids are almost human-like in appearance: even to the point where they might be able to have a conversation with a human being without raising suspicion. Provided they were careful in hiding their true identity, of course, as university experiments with 'Katie' demonstrated some years ago.

"The hypothetical class six, however, takes this principle one step further: it supposes the existence of an android who is indistinguishable from a human being in almost every respect possible — even in rudimentary field tests. It supposes an I.E.B. made of non-metallic components — or at least, in concentrations similar to what a human being has in their body. It supposes an I.E.B. of similar weight and proportion to a human being, with synthetic skin, and an artificially grown skeleton. It supposes an I.E.B. with unique fingerprints, tongue prints, and blood-alcohol levels. And, of course, it's premise is entirely absurd."

Alex furrowed his brow. "You mean to say impossible, Mrs. President?"

"Oh, heavens no, not impossible. If there's anything I've learned from my exposure to that field, it's that scarce little is impossible. It's quite conceivable that somebody might build an android body to such a specification. Saltwater can conduct electricity perfectly well, just as the human brain itself demonstrates. It's just that such an android's existence would be tortured, impractical, and short — its very body works within such stark limitations, while deliberately ignoring the advantages that a conventional android body might otherwise have at its disposal. Such a construction would exist only as a novelty, or perhaps as a display piece in an exhibition. Opponents to the I.E.B. civil rights movement often cite the possibility of a class six as a dangerous threat to national security, or as an excuse to further the opposition against the development of I.E.B. integration with society.

"But by itself, the postulated class six serves no purpose beyond acting as a scary hypothetical. Its very name might as well be a non-sequitur. After all, an I.E.B. that can pose as a human being is no more dangerous than any other human being is. Its capabilities are even severely limited with the additional burden of faux biology that serves no purpose other than to act as an imitation."

Silence filled the room. Alex and Derek both turned away, staring towards the center of the table.

Fischer sighed and set down her coffee cup to address the need for reassurance. "Listen. I have little doubt that the voting masses will come to the same conclusions as we have today concerning this subject. Despite the economic struggles this term has brought, we've managed to keep the American population well fed and protected — which is more than several other nations can say about themselves in recent years. And while those who are susceptible to scare tactics like this will continue to vote for the same party they always have, I imagine that most voting citizens are finding that outlandish claims made by the I.E.B. opposition are starting to wear thin. Overall, I have my doubts that attack ads like this pose any threat to my reelection. Are we clear?"

Several affirmative nods and murmurs filled the room.

"Excellent. Now, on to the next item on our agenda..."

Chapter 13

Project Log Day 458

"But I don't want to look like a human, Robert. I'm proud of how I look and who I am. Aren't you too?"

Robert sighed and shook his head. Katie was a beautiful person — she really was. It wasn't just her appearance, either: already, just about every one of her parts had been replaced at least once so far, with the exception of her central processor. And through all the time they'd spent together, with all the changes that had befallen her, he had genuinely grown fond of who she had become.

It pained him to see her upset. But it was too late to back out of the commitment now.

"Katie, we've been over this with Doctor Sarah. The plans have been made, and you agreed with them. Your development has plateaued. There isn't significantly more you can learn from your interactions with the team — especially from within the confines of the testing area. It's time for you to venture out into the real world for a change, even if it's for just a little while."

Katie glanced at the various synthetic faces that adorned the wall, each one mounted across the skull of an endoskeleton identical to her own. The array, provided by the bio-synthetic department, was gifted to her as a selection of new possible appearances for when the big week came.

Robert was right, of course — they had already established the procedure with her in advance, and the plans were just recently announced across the school's bulletin system for all to see.

The announcement itself was simple, yet vague by design. It claimed that during the welcome week on university campus, there would be an android from the department walking freely on campus among the student population.

It would be indistinguishable from a human person in every manner of everyday interaction. No information was to be disclosed detailing whether it would be male or female in appearance, or even if it were to change its appearance regularly. Since Katie's creation, she had developed to the point of being able to replicate movement and conversation in a manner consistent with a human: nobody would be able to distinguish her based off her speech patterns or facial expressions. Tests had already been performed on a physical replica of Katie's body. Her synthetic skin disguise would be sufficient at masking the sound of her servos while maintaining appropriate flexibility and temperature.

To everybody else, Katie would appear as a first-year transfer student. She had already established a portfolio of possible alibis and had practiced reciting them to perfection. Nobody would question a new student appearing or disappearing from the crowd during the first week of class. Students were already expected to treat each other with a friendly demeanor during welcome week, and surveys reported a nearly universal sense of fervent anticipation to the possibility of a secret android.

Overall, it was just short of foolproof: Katie would be able to interact with others and gain valuable new experiences. She'd be able to do so in a natural setting without crowds gathering around her and giving unwarranted attention. And it acted as a promotional stunt for the school, securing additional admissions and advertising to donors, while justifying the program's funding.

But it still felt wrong to her.

"I want them to accept me for who I am, Robert. I don't want to be fawned over or questioned. I don't like that I'm exceptional just because of how I look or behave. I just want to be treated like any other person."

Robert grimaced somewhat, resting his elbows on his knees, and letting his hands hang. "I know, Katie. I'm sorry that it's this way too. But the fact of the matter is that you're not normal. You are exceptional. It can't be helped. And nobody outside the staff of this research program has ever laid eyes upon somebody quite like you before. You couldn't expect me to lie to you and say otherwise. Could you?"

Katie lowered her head. Robert pursed his lips. He thought quickly and reached out to tilt her chin up. "Hey…"

Her eyes clicked into place, meeting his.

"Don't forget why you're doing this, Katie. It's more than just an enriching experience for you. It's more than just a way to keep the university afloat for another year. We're doing this for a greater reason: we're looking to try to make this something normal. We're doing this so that one day, I.E.B.s like you can walk down a street and be treated as though it's an everyday occurrence. You're the first step in achieving that kind of world – and through that, you have the power to make anything out of it. And personally, I don't think I'd have anybody else taking on that task. I wouldn't have it any other way. Alright?"

The look of despair left her eyes, if only for a moment.

"Alright."

The big day came.

Orientation groups were formed out in the field adjacent to the dorms, each wearing their own colored lanyards to distinguish their tour group. An auto pulled up to the front of the building and found a parking spot.

Robert turned off the motor and turned to Katie. He smiled. She didn't.

"Hey. Everything will be alright. Boring, even. You can do this. Okay?"

She nodded. He was partly right – everything presented to her today would be old news. It was all the little details that people didn't realize they were betraying that she'd be paying special attention to today.

Hesitant to leave the comfort of familiar company, she finally opened the door and stepped out into the warm afternoon, surveying the new sunlit world around her — a campus entirely different from the nighttime world she was otherwise familiar with. She looked back to Robert, forced a gentle smile, and waved him goodbye. He waved back and ordered the auto to drive off.

And there, at last, she stood.

For the first time in her life, Katie was completely alone.

She toyed with her new hair: blond, and reaching down to her middle back. She almost couldn't believe that Doctor Sarah was initially willing to donate the hair from her own head for the cause.

She brought her left hand to her right arm and ran her fingertips across the skin. A pale shade: a color that radiated the most light and heat, while further helping to mask her appearance.

She adjusted her scarf to better hide her neck. An item of her own selection, along with pants, blouse, messenger bag, and a thick jacket. Both Robert and Sarah had respected her desire to exhibit freedom in choosing her own colors, and had provided only minimal suggestions in her final look.

Everything was in perfect order.

She was petrified anyway.

She pulled out her phone — a unit borrowed from Sarah — and brought up Robert's contact. Even through her internal panic, she praised herself for making a point of using it, rather than using her own internal wireless connection. Just like a human would.

Katie: I can't do this. I'm too scared.

It didn't take long for Robert to respond.

Robert: You absolutely can do this. You've had practice, your visuals have passed blind tests, and you have the team watching through your eyes at the ready to give you advice. You don't have to spend the whole day here. The more data the better, but ultimately, you're the one choosing when to opt out.

She knew it already, but, having somebody else affirm it made her feel a little better.

Katie: Alright. Here I go. Wish me luck.

As she put her phone away in the messenger bag, a group chat prompt appeared from within the internal messenger from Robert, Sarah, Brian, and a few others.

Team: Good luck, Katie! We believe in you!

Out of pride for her own fear, she tried her hardest not to chuckle. The tour was the single most harrowing thing she had experienced in her short life.

As she walked alongside humans — other humans! Other humans that she'd never seen before, and might never see again! — she listened idly to the tour guide announce information about the various faculties provided on campus. She already knew everything but pretended her hardest to listen anyways. She even began counting the tiny mistakes the guide made about various campus facts. Her internal panic subsided, if not only a little.

For a while, things seemed to be going alright. Stable. Manageable.

Halfway through the first leg of the tour, as the group made their way through the quad, she glimpsed a small crowd of students gathered on top of a hill around a card table. She turned her head and leaned in, venturing to look a little more closely at the collective. They looked mostly like second or third-year students, with the ones seated behind the table each wielding a stethoscope and a breathalyzer.

The banner that hung across the card table read, 'Are You the Secret Android?'

Panic shot through her. Katie turned back to the tour guide and did her best to hide herself a little deeper within the depths of the crowd.

"Hey. Glad I'm not the only person who was creeped out by them."

It took all of Katie's self-control to keep herself from whipping around like a frightened animal. She turned in the direction which the voice came from. Walking alongside her was a girl, maybe nineteen years old. She had darker skin, and wore her short black hair in a bob cut. Her face held a faint smile with droopy eyelids — an almost bored expression.

When words failed her, Katie reflexively pushed the burden onto the stranger. "Pardon?"

The girl nodded towards the table on the hill. "The testers. Up on the hill. I don't think they should be allowed to do that. Not without a signature on a health form, anyways. I wouldn't be surprised if University Police got on their case at any moment now. What do you think about it, anyways?"

"What, the android?"

"Yeah, that. Exciting, isn't it?"

Katie struggled to avoid bias. She ultimately resolved to take a tangential approach.

"I dunno. I kind of doubt that what they're advertising is the whole truth. Maybe it's all just a hoax to try to get more applicants. Maybe there is no android."

The girl thought for a bit and shrugged. "I mean, that's a fair point. They were kind of vague about it. As a counterpoint, what if there are multiple androids, and we've all been led to believe there's just the one?"

Feeling a little bit more comfortable, Katie exercised a smile with the stranger. "My name's

Katie, by the way. You?"

"Jennifer. Call me Jen, though. I'm a bio major. What about you?"

"I'm mechanical engineering." As she spoke, she could already almost hear the rare sound of Sarah's laughter from the other side of the screen.

Jennifer smiled. "That's cool. Certainly a lot of potential there. I'm looking to get into the biomechanical field. You living in the dorms?"

She was quick to come up with a white lie. "No. I'll be off campus with some friends." Granted, it wasn't entirely false.

"That's cool. Hey, you wanna sit down and talk after this leg of the tour? During the lunch period?"

Katie tensed up, but it didn't take long for her mind to consider the possibilities. This was her chance to have a more comfortable conversation with a singular individual.

"I don't usually eat lunch. I wouldn't mind sitting down and talking with you, though."

Jennifer smiled. "That works too."

After a few hours, a handful of conversations of a similar caliber, a lunch period, and the welcoming sight of University Police disbanding the students at the table on the hill, Katie quietly broke away from the tour and made her way back to building seventeen.

As she walked through the familiar halls, the feeling of comfort and safety returned to her. She walked through the final set of doors that separated the outside world from her cozy testing area and was greeted with a round of applause from the staff. Robert stepped out from the crowd and wrapped his arms around her.

"You performance was exceptional, Katie," said Doctor Sarah, stepping forward, holding a tablet. "The data you've collected has already created marked changes in your development. If it's any comfort to you, we've scanned over your facial recognition feeds. We've found that in all likelihood, not a soul you met today held even the passing suspicion that you were anything but human."

Katie beamed at first, but her heart sank. It didn't escape Robert's notice.

"Hey. What's wrong?"

She fumbled with the words. "It's…. well, if the testing is over for today… Can I step out of the skin, please?"

The lab fell silent, save for the soft hum of the machines scattered about the room.

"It feels… well, it feels like I'm lying, and I don't like it. It doesn't even need to be completely removed. Even if I keep my face, or if it was just a visible indicator light on the side of my neck, or any other way for me to distinguish myself — if it makes others feel more comfortable with interacting with me here in the lab, I don't mind wearing the skin. But the thought that, by wearing the disguise in full, I can lie so convincingly that others might forget about what I really am…. well, honestly, that prospect frightens me."

Robert thought hard, stroking his goatee, before turning to Sarah. She shrugged and stammered. "I see no reason not to. The fact of the matter is, you aren't human, Katie. And I know it's a little hypocritical for us to say this after today's events, but you really shouldn't be expected to identify as something you aren't — especially towards those who are closest to you. Why don't we go ahead and get you into a more honest state? If not just for now."

Katie's smile returned. "Thanks, Sarah."

Chapter 14

Today was the day of Randall's third meeting with A6.

The last time that Randall came to visit, he had experienced a less than enjoyable encounter with a couple of androids after getting off the bus. A6 agreed that it would be better to meet Randall at the station outside of his complex before walking him over to its domicile.

Randall wasn't blind to the other androids watching them walk along, as they made their way to the flat. While this was an I.E.B. only community, it wasn't too often that he came across one where the occasional human visitor was viewed as this peculiar. Or unwelcome. He wasn't sure which.

A number of the mechanical turned away and went back to their business, one after another, as they passed them by. Randall resolved to test a hypothesis.

"Hey, A6?"

A6 was silent. Then, it turned its head at a sharp angle to face him. "Sorry, yes?"

At that exact moment, the next android they passed bumped into Randall's shoulder as they walked on by.

This supported Randall's suspicion: since having entered the community, he hadn't heard a single spoken word. A6 was holding direct conversations with each of the robots they passed through shortwave radio signals. Swiftclick, it was called. Allegedly, to excuse or apologize for the presence of the alien invader.

"Well," said Randall, working to resume his train of thought, "I guess I was just curious about why it was you elected to outfit yourself with a class four body, anyways. I find that just about every android has their reasons. What's yours?"

"It's a straightforward reason – most humans are pretty shit." As they spoke, a class one robot wheeled by and overheard the conversation in passing. It emitted a chattering snicker, and out of his nervousness, Randall couldn't help but smile – even if he was aware of the ridicule. A6 ignored it and continued. "Really, the only ones worth talking to are the same ones brave enough to look past the appearance."

"You really think so, huh."

"Yep."

Randall's mind went to mohawks and spiked leather and torn jeans. "I can understand that. There are humans that are like that too. And it's not an altogether uncommon reason for those who do choose class fours. I guess my default response is to raise concern over opportunity. Don't you worry that it closes door on chances you could otherwise have? Chances provided by people who aren't otherwise resilient enough to see past it all?"

A6 shrugged. "Yeah, well fuck those people, then," it said with a nonchalant tone. "I gave it a lot of thought, and I think I place a higher value on my principles than I do a sense of cheap comfort offered to me by a suit with a fake grin. I don't have very many needs as it is, anyway."

"And that's fair. Nobody wants to have to put up with that. And I'll be darned if I'm going to try to change you over that."

Though he didn't show it with his face, his walk betrayed him. A6 beamed with pride – just a little – despite its scowl. "Damn right. See, that's why you're one of the few tolerable humans, Randall. That's why I don't mind you."

"Well thank you kindly."

"Sure thing."

"Still, though," he said holding his paperwork with one hand while opening the door to the apartment with the other, "What happens when you're put into a situation where something important depends on that sort of thing? A hearing during a trial? A job opportunity? Or in a life-or-death situation? Aren't you a slave one way or another? Confined either to personal dishonesty, or the judgment of others?"

A6 grew uncomfortable but didn't hesitate to produce a pragmatic solution "Well then. Guess we need more people in power who are less likely to judge solely on appearance," he announced down to Randall from the top of the stairs.

"Merely wishing upon a star that other horrible people just magically become better people doesn't help much of anything. At least from I've learned so far in life," said Randall, catching his breath at the top of the flight. A6 opened the door and they both walked in. "If anything, a systematized solution, accepted by society, is what usually provides the best results. Don't forget the impact that the I.E.B. justice system reformation has already had."

A6 turned sharply and pointed a bony finger at his face. "Don't you get me started on that."

Randall gave an exasperated shrug and elected to hold his tongue. A6 lowered his finger and the moment passed.

"Speaking of which, we probably ought to go over the legal work. Just to say that we did it."

The paperwork was done quickly enough. Randall had already gone out of his way to fill in most of the data ahead of time. It took a quick conversation, an agreement on what was discussed, a log on the time they had spent discussing it, and a signature.

Randall buried the papers away under his clipboard and sighed. "Well, that just about wraps up my work here. If there's anything else you'd like to discuss, you're free to. Otherwise, if you want me gone, that's fine too."

A6 thought for a moment. "I might have a question for you."

"Yeah? What's that?"

A6 leaned back on its joints and placed its hands on the back of its head. "Have you ever considered running for public office, Randall?"

The very thought made Randall scoff without hesitation. "Yes. Yes, I have sometimes. It's often thereafter overruled by the considerations of taking a long walk on a short pier. The latter would certainly be far more consequential."

"Really now. I'd vote for you in a heartbeat."

Randall smirked. "You don't have a heart, and certainly not one that beats."

A6 raised a mechanical eyebrow. "Right. And you probably haven't walked off a pier at any point in your life either."

A few childhood memories danced about his mind for just a moment. "Oh, you might be surprised. We did have piers back then, and I like to think we made the most of them."

"I am being serious, though. I think a lot of people would see you as somebody who went into a flawed system and did his part to improve it. Especially with all the I.E.B.s you've been forced to deal with vouching for you. Besides that, there have been politicians who've sought loftier goals and have come from even more humble positions. Lyndon B. Johnson was a school teacher. He claimed that was what part of what compelled him to make a change, if ever an ounce of truth escaped his lips."

Randall hesitated at the thought. "It wouldn't do any good. Successful politicians are the sorts who step on the toes of others to stay in power. I'm not that sort of person."

"You don't have to be. There's a reason single-issue political parties exist, and a reason why I even vouch for them sometimes. I believe that it's never throwing your vote away, no matter which way it goes down. Even if their leaders have no actual chance of winning, that doesn't mean they shouldn't run. The more that people vote for them, the more that major political parties pay attention and work to adopt their principles. Sure. You might not win office as senator or governor. But if you get enough people shouting and screaming and rioting on your behalf for the change they deserve, then it pressures those in power to undermine you and adopt your positions to stay in power. Sure, it's fake as fuck. But it's the easiest way to make the change you want."

Randall rested his chin on his fist. "Trust me, I've figured that much out myself. I just don't think it'd be worth my time and effort to do that."

"And I disagree. If there's ever a person who might be able to accomplish it, it'd be you. The reason you took on this job is because you wanted to make a positive impact on the interactions between I.E.B. - kind and human-kind. Isn't that right?"

"Well, sure, but-"

"Just how many of the I.E.B.s you've consulted with do you think might say that you've left a positive impact on them?"

Randall stammered. Damned if he did, damned if he didn't. He tried a humble approach. "I really can't tell. I'd like to say most of them, but that's never an accurate statement, really, is it?"

"From all the thousands of visitations you've made over dozens of years, with hundreds of disgruntled chunks of metal like me, surely, some of them must have thought well of you. You have any idea how much noise hundreds of androids, hundreds of I.E.B.s of every shape or size, can make over an issue they feel strongly about? More than a few of us are afraid. Or passionate. Or desperate. I worry about it all the time. Maybe tomorrow, I'll fuck up. Or it might not even be anything I did – I might just end up in the wrong place at the wrong time, and I'll end up spending the rest of my life in confinement as a sleeping processor on the shelf of a police station. Sure, it's better than conforming to human assimilation, but it's still not ideal."

Randall looked down at his clipboard, lost in thought. His eyes wandered up and down the fingers on his right hand. "I'll think it over."

"Think it over all you want. I'm sure that'll make the change we need happen so much faster."

Randall winced. "You really are a bit of a smarmy asshole, aren't you?"

A6 seemed to be proud of itself for having finally fished some profanity out of Randall. "Oh, beyond question. I'll be preparing a list of a few people who might be willing to support the efforts. You let me know when you want to throw your hat in the ring. Your ambassador history is publicly accessible, right?"

Chapter 15

Project Log Day 460

It was the third day of Katie's on-campus tour portion of welcome week. Though she'd made a few friends along the way, she spent most of the walks talking to Jen.

"….but anyways, that's just my own opinion on the closure of Pudong. I've been yammering enough, I'm sure. What do you think?"

There was sudden resistance. A slight tug from her left side. A loud tearing noise. Her right arm whipped around to catch herself, palm over the spot in question.

She looked down and peered through the gap in her fingers and found a large tear in her right arm. As her mind raced through her personal denial, the unrelenting truth emerged.

This was bad.

The tear was larger than her own flat palm could cover on its own. It wasn't terribly deep, but just deep enough to expose the metallic hinges and wires that ran through her from within. A portion of her skin hung intact — longer and thinner than any human skin could reasonably manage. And she did not bleed.

Much to her horror — and despite her subconscious expectations — the world kept on going around her, somehow. Katie stood in the middle of the quad, holding her arm, as people near and far went on with their day, passing her by.

A voice somewhere in the back of her mind told her to cover the tear with the university sweatshirt she had wrapped around her waist. Another voice told her that casually putting it on would be the more normal course of action – just let the long sleeve hide it for now. Another voice still made mention that if she just stood there doing nothing, then maybe everything would work out on its own somehow.

She stood petrified.

A faraway voice called for her name. Jennifer's voice. She must have broken out of her monologue and noticed by now that Katie had lagged behind. "Katie? Are you alright? Your arm-"

"Holy fuck, guys! It's the android!"

It didn't take long for a small crowd to form. Digital eyes of all sorts were pointed in her direction — phones, cameras, integrated glasses — each with its own flickering light that flashed across her. As more people gathered, she forced herself to undo the sweatshirt and pulled it over herself, backing away from the growing crowd.

But it was too late: the facade was broken, and the flashes persisted, disconnecting the excited voices from the faces, behind a flickering wall of bright light that threatened to consume her.

"Look! Another one! The boy with the black hair!"

Puzzled, Katie turned her head towards the direction of the voice and saw Jennifer. She stood with an awestruck expression on her face and was pointing to an individual that stood tangential to the crowd. The doubt wasn't much, but it was enough — especially for those who were late to the event and hadn't yet caught a glimpse of the tear. Heads and cameras turned away, and a few people moved. As the crowd shifted, Katie felt a hard tug at her wrist pulling her away from her unwanted audience.

"Alright. Where do you need to get to? Where's someplace you'll be safe?" Katie turned and found Jennifer pulling her away. Even after running only a few yards together, was already almost out of breath, and only managed the questions between gasps.

"Building seventeen. East side of Campus," Katie spoke through her daze. She realized that Jennifer had swallowed her fib from a few days earlier and was leading them west towards the campus maglev station. "Away from the trains."

Jennifer nodded and turned left around the next corner, away from the growing voices of the crowd. Katie picked up her pace and began carrying her own unnatural weight, and Jennifer let go of her wrist.

The personal messages from inside Katie's dialogue box were exploding. She closed out the voices, but even as she fell into a natural sprint alongside Jen, she couldn't help but feel an overwhelming sense of guilt. More than ever before, she felt like a liar. A traitor. A complete fraud, exposed to the only person from the outside world she'd grown close to.

Katie tripped as they approached building seventeen and ran up the steps, losing one of her shoes. The faint sound of the University Police sirens and distorted speaker voices echoed across the campus. Jennifer stopped at the top of the stairs, catching her breath with her hands on her knees. Finally, she looked at Katie. "Is the damage stable? Are you alright?"

In all the excitement, she hadn't even considered it. She performed a quick calibration test. Everything came back positive. "It's only superficial. It's fine. Really."

"Think you'll be okay from here?" Katie nodded. Something caught her eye: she looked up to find an auto with 'community services' written on its side wheeling around the corner, red and blue lights flashing. Her heart sank, and she looked back to Jennifer. "What about you? Will you be alright?"

Jennifer shrugged it off, a hurt smile on her face. "I think I'll be okay. I'm sure the officers will have more than a few questions for me, but with any luck, it'll be better than being torn apart by a crowd of curious students."

But Katie started imagining the worst, and with that, it all became too much. "Jen…. I'm so sorry for everything. I'm sorry for lying to you and for dragging you into this and for-"

Jennifer closed her eyes and raised a hand. "Don't be. It might be hard for you, but I want you to know that I think I understand. And I certainly don't think any less of you for it. I wouldn't have done any of what I did just now if I didn't mean that."

"I hope I get to see you again, Jen. I really do."

"I hope so too. But I don't have any expectations."

Katie felt the need to babble, coupled with the awkward feeling of having nothing to say. She heard car doors slamming. Campus officers were running up the steps.

"Jen…. Thank you."

It pained her. Katie always had a hard time saying goodbye, ever since she learned what it meant. She even struggled to say it to the regular faculty she knew she'd be seeing again the next morning. The word 'forever' haunted the back of her mind. In that moment, she hated it with every fiber of her being.

Jennifer nodded solemnly, before turning around to sit down on the top step, facing the officers. Katie turned back towards the building and walked back inside, closing the door behind her, and ignoring the commands barked at her by the officers. The world went quiet again, interrupted only by the clicking of both her feet against the marble floor.

"No. Absolutely not."

Doctor Wilson was struggling to keep her voice at equilibrium – low enough to keep her composure, yet high enough to be heard over the dozens of phone calls and message alerts that the I.E.B. department was receiving. It hadn't taken long for a video feed of the incident to circulate, and it had taken even less time for the department's contact information to fall into the hands of anybody curious enough to want it. She cleared her throat and continued.

"This was a serious mistake, Katie. We're all grateful enough that it was appropriately contained and that you're back in our hands in one piece, but the fact of the matter is that you had a serious compromise to your own safety. And seeing how the community reacted, I don't think we can afford to risk putting you in harm's way like that again. Not anytime soon, anyways — and certainly not with you wearing a blatant indicator light for all to see."

Katie's face knotted up into a scowl, much to Doctor Wilson's surprise. Katie didn't want to back down from this — and if there was anything she'd learned from their months developing her, it was that when Katie had strong feelings about something, very little could be done to convince her otherwise.

"That's unfair and you know it, Wilson," spat Katie. "Factually speaking, I'm collecting more valuable data than ever before, I've received no worse physical harm than usual, and the university is getting positive attention unlike any it's ever had. It's entirely possible for us to play this off as a part of the publicity stunt and continue the testing unhindered tomorrow, right on schedule, with a new disguise from the synthetic biology department's collection."

Doctor Wilson slumped down in her office chair and rubbed her temples.

"Fine. We'll talk it over as a group. Even if we can come to an agreement, you'll need to pick not just a new skin, but a new voice, and maybe even a new personality. And we're certainly not letting you out there without a member of the team nearby, at all times. Alright?"

Katie opened her mouth but found no reasonable objections. "Fine. Can I make one last request?"

"What is it, Katie," asked Sarah, letting her hands fall to her lap.

"Can it be Robert?"

Chapter 16

"A6 honestly thinks I should run for office. Can you believe it? It genuinely thinks I could make a difference."

As Randall walked down the street, Sally walked with her four identical iterations together in a perfectly ordered stride. They could have effortlessly given the impression of a small army of four soldiers marching information, if it weren't for the fact that the first two in line occasionally broke sync to kick at any one of the random rocks or twigs that adorned the broken pavement.

That, and the fact that there weren't very many armies of pink androids out there in what was left of the world.

Her first body shrugged, and her third body spoke up. "Well, sure I can believe it. It told me, after all." Randall swore under his breath, and Sally did her best not to giggle. A6 had snitched on him. No doubt, it had already conversed with hundreds of the other I.E.B.s he had served in his prior years as ambassador. He raked away at his mind and tried to remember whether that act violated any laws of confidentiality between them, but the rules always became complicated.

Especially for beings that spoke with one other at the speed of light across time and space.

Sally noticed Randall's face darken and turned to him with a more serious expression. "I mean, what's wrong with that? Whether or not you choose to pursue it, I still think you're just the right kind of person to make a good representative. And besides that, the fact of the matter is that very few people right now would be likely to vote an android into office, much less any other kind of I.E.B. Unless they happened to be a Class six and nobody knew it, of course."

Her second body piped in seamlessly after the third had finished. "But somebody who's worked in the community with I.E.B.s, somebody who knew about the inner workings of the bureaucracy and had a history as a civil servant…" Her voice switched to her first body again, "It really isn't hard to make a case for that, is it? The campaign almost runs itself."

When Randall's face failed to lighten up in the least, Sally started to fidget like a timid child. They walked together in silence through the broken suburbs – Sally's request for today's meeting – and took in the landscape around them. The sun was setting, and the orange light cast a warm glow across the overgrown landscape. The leaves and creepers, a passing mechanical squirrel, the occasional electric tree – they'd even become a part of the vast cityscape, growing in alleys and on the roofs of skyscrapers. But in the cities, they were well ordered. In the suburbs, there was no question over which the dominant force of life was.

After an uncomfortable silence and an exasperated sigh, he replied, "A representative? I can't do that. I'm not an exceptional person. I'm just trying my hardest to be a model citizen. To bring connections between individual-"

Randall stopped himself in his tracks and looked over at each of the Sallys and found four identical faces looking back at him with a smug leer, hands on their hips. ".... Fine. Or not so individual... people. Look, if I really strike you as somebody fit to govern a populace, then one of us is making a serious misjudgment. I couldn't shoulder that burden, anyway. I have enough on my plate. Enough of a struggle getting a meal in my mouth by the end of the day."

"Alright, well two things," said her first body, before her second body added, "One: it's not just one of us making this judgment. It's me,"

"and me,"

"and me!"

"and me,"

"...and a good couple of other people. Most of the I.E.B.s you've worked with before. Especially the ones who credit you as the reason they've been successfully integrated into society. You've changed lives before, Randall. You've already demonstrated your potential.

"Secondly, we've already seen a vast history full of people who'd gotten up every morning to shoulder that particular sort of burden, before asking for seconds by filing for reelection. If they can, you can too. And you wouldn't be alone in your efforts, either. Far from it. You'd have your cabinet and supervisors helping you through, along with the support of countless voters. Nobody does it alone, and you can't expect to do so either."

"Countless," scoffed Randall. "That number's a little optimistic"

"You get my point," picked up the fourth Sally, without missing a beat. "And beyond that, we all have faith that you'd be able to see through it with greater success than others could. That's not just me. You have a better understanding of our wants and needs that others who haven't been privileged with your perspective. You'd be able to supervise the orders to distribute the means to keep us alive. Electricity, or maintenance. Or our status as citizens. Our legal defense. Our right to produce offspring, even. To build the lives we want to build without obstruction. You coul-"

"Well then maybe I don't want to," Randall spat at her.

The tone of his voice surprised even him. Each of the Sally's stopped short, some a little faster than others, causing the two behind in line to bump into the ones ahead. He stammered. "Maybe it's just… too much for me to have to think about. Too much pressure. Or too dangerous. But it's not ever something I've told myself that I want to do."

Sally gazed up at him with four poignant sets of eyes. "Maybe you really don't want to do that, Randall. I can understand that. I can respect that.

"But maybe we need you, Randall."

Randall's job required a lot of conscious interpretation. Many androids gave off an appearance that could easily lend itself to the formation of prejudices. His active participation in their lives demanded that he look past that.

But even he was unprepared for the sight of four wide-eyed, pink-haired androids, out in the middle of a quiet suburban avenue, staring up at him with this level of desperation.

".... What?"

"You're a civil servant, Randall. I can't imagine the government pays you any extraordinary amount by any measure. That's not the reason you chose this line of work, and perhaps more importantly, stuck with it for so long. I'm convinced that you selected it because you genuinely believe you're doing good for others. Especially those who desperately need it.

"And that's fine and well. I wouldn't be one to push you. Especially after all you've done so far to get me, and so many others, the integration and understanding we so desperately need.

"But the fact of the matter is, there are very few people like you out there. Sure, there are people who are bothered enough to vote or to donate to a cause. But to find a qualified individual who's willing to go out there and participate in the workings of the problem at their own expense is a rare find indeed.

"I guess what we're getting after is, well...."

Sally's four identical voices spoke in a haunting unison. "Maybe we need you, Randall."

Randall said nothing. The orange of the sun had finished its spread across the sky and was lending itself to grey. All was quiet. He thought back to a time when there wasn't so much silence. When the sound of a passing car, or a distant airplane lent itself as a means of breaking the tension of these moments. A white noise to counter the discomfort, to ease the blows. But all there was now was silence.

He lowered himself down to the curb and placed his elbows on his knees. Sally stood there, her eyes glowing softly in the evening. He shook his head, burying it into the sides of his folded arms.

"Fine. I'll do it."

One of Sally's forms walked over to him and placed a hand on his back.

"I ought to say thank you, Randall Anderson. But I know it wouldn't ever do you justice."

Chapter 17

Project Log Day 527

"We have to leave, Katie, and we're leaving right this minute. No questions."

Katie made no effort in hiding her agitation, nor her skepticism. This was fine by Robert — in fact, he might not have even noticed if she hadn't been vocal about it. Presently, he was too occupied with the frantic task of packing up his papers and tablets in the cardboard boxes he had brought with him to his office.

"That can't be right, Robert," she spoke with stern defiance. "You're lying to me. Don't do that, it's frightening. Stop it."

Katie must be pretty angry, he concluded. She had mastered emulating conversational interactions, but when a disruption to the humdrum of everyday life reared its ugly head, when things fell out of place, everything crumbled for her, and she retreated back to the familiarity of an analytic response.

"Well, tough," spat Robert, as he shoved a final stack of papers into a box and closing the lid. His hand passed over an analog counter, presently marked five hundred and twenty seven, and for a brief moment, he had to suppress his urge to smash it to pieces. He turned to the next stack, and that's when Katie caught his wrist, bringing it to a halt in midair, his hand hovering just above his desk.

Robert's heart stopped. Katie wasn't equipped with the strongest hardware he had ever worked with, but she was still far more capable than she might let on, and the sudden snatch caught him off guard. He might have jerked away from her, or shoved her to the ground, or any other number of other violent reactions.

But instead, he looked up at her. A glare at first, complete with the expectation of her scowling snarl staring right back at him. But then when he saw her expression of worry, her silent plea for reassurance…

Robert's shoulders drooped. She let go of him, and he slumped back in his chair.

"Alright, Katie. Go on. Message Dr. Wilson. Ask her, if you don't believe me."

Katie blinked once. She stood above him, arms at her sides, her fists balled up tight. Several minutes passed as she stood, waiting for a reply with unusual patience. Then her eyes widened. Her mouth opened. And although she lacked the capacity for it, Robert had no doubt that tears would be rolling down her face this very moment, were she capable of doing so.

"I'm sorry, Katie," whispered Robert, looking away. "I'm upset too."

"Why?"

"It's always been a threat to our funding. We had contingency plans, but none of them big enough for something as immense as the entire department getting the ax. And especially not this suddenly." Robert clenched his eyes, lowered his forehead into his palms and let his mind wander back to all the research they had prepared for — all the new directions they had planned to explore. Katie pulled up a chair and folded her hands in her lap.

"….I wasn't good enough, was I."

"No Katie, it had nothing to do with you. You performed above and beyond every expectation. There was nothing you had control over that you didn't excel at."

Katie peered at Robert with eyes that inquired deeper. He tried to avoid her gaze, but he couldn't help but continue.

"The entire university's going under, Katie. There's nothing we could have done about it — our division was just a meager hope to the contrary. It's government-funding, is what it is. Current administration's making cuts that donors and investors and on-campus advertisement alone can't cover. They won't admit it, unless it's behind closed doors. But they're cutting programs one by one to buy time. Pretty shortly they'll stop accepting student applications. They'll come up with some horseshit to make themselves sound hopeful and progressive, I'm sure. Online teaching's what they were talking about. As though that's really going to be the next big thing. But it's done," spat Robert in defeat. "We're all done for here."

Katie's gaze drifted to the carpeted floor. She shuffled in her seat. "What…. what will become of me, then?"

For a while, Robert considered lying. Not because he wanted to, but just because the truth hurt so much. He remembered the hours spent in President Henry's office, debating the matter. They'd begun by arguing over the current trajectory of the institute. Perhaps a merger could save it. Or an aggressive marketing campaign. Then, the topic shifted to whether there was another project or department he could be transferred to. Somewhere where he might have some use, where his talents might be fruitful.

Then the conversation turned to Katie. Under the current regulation, the hardware she occupied was campus property. It'd need to be repossessed, sold to pay off costs. Just thinking back on that, just hearing those words again in his mind made him sweat, made him clench his jaw.

Oh, how he pleaded. He had made arguments from his very heart. Words of passion that spoke of her very nature, her thoughts and feelings, of what she had come to mean for the campus community in her brief time here. But each of these words fell on deaf ears. There was simply nothing to be done about it — Henry had made up his mind.

He was disgusted with himself when he thought back upon it — maybe with time he'd come to rationalize it, just to help him sleep at night — but he had even offered to buy her from his clutches. Even in the moment, he felt horrified with himself. That he would stoop so low as to try to speak the man's language. That he would, if not just for a moment, treat her like she was property. Worth so little. Worth only the sum of her parts.

He blinked and turned to Katie, looking into her eyes.

He couldn't lie to her. She was too smart for that. In some respects, she was smarter than anybody else on the team. No. Lying wouldn't do.

So, he resolved to tell the truth.

Carefully edited truth.

"We'll take care of you, Katie. So long as that's what you desire. Me and Sarah and Brian are already onboard wholeheartedly. A few others on the team are willing to dedicate their own time, too. Even Jennifer would be happy to see you again."

Katie nodded, and some of the worry left her eyes. "You really mean it?"

"Absolutely," said Robert. His mind turned to the University Police Department. For all he knew, somebody had intercepted them. Maybe there was a rat. Maybe they were coming for him this very minute. "But we need to get moving. We can't stop now. I've already filed a letter of resignation. Next step is to clear the office and grab an auto to take us home. We can figure it out as a group from there. That sound alright?"

"That sounds wonderful. Will everybody be there?"

"Hey. Don't believe me. Ask Sarah yourself," he said, shelving his tablets side by side in a dedicated box.

Katie turned her eyes up. Her indicator light flashed. Then she smiled. Robert tightened his lips into a grimace. Thank goodness Dr. Wilson was in on the charade.

"You wanna help me out by gathering your things?""I can't honestly think of anything I'd like more."

Although Robert smiled back, his heart sank in his chest. He could only hope that when she got a better understanding of the bigger picture that she'd be forgiving of him. For now, a return to stability would be enough.

Chapter 18

"Hey, Randall. I think you got your first letter."

Robert closed the door behind him and walked into the main room with a small, rectangular envelope in his hands. Randall couldn't stop himself from smiling as he got up from his chair to retrieve it. "Well, would you look at that. An actual letter."

It didn't take long before A6 let out an impulsive remark. "What's a letter?"

Randall raised an eyebrow at him. Robert snickered. A6 stiffened and began researching the matter on the local network. One of Sally's iterations let out a light squeal, while another raced off, and yet another barely whispered, "Oh goodness, I'll need to show it my stamp collection!"

Katie glanced at Sally. "You brought your stamp collection. Really. Honestly, with all the luggage you brought over, why am I actually surprised?"

It had been two days since Randall had announced his campaign for Mayor at the university

campus, and about five days since A6, Sally, Robert and Katie had all agreed to move in with Randall for the duration of the election. Yet despite all that time, Sally still seemed to be in the process of settling into her guest room. When she had first arrived in her own auto last week, it had appeared as though she had brought along with her just about everything from her own home. Even with four of her own bodies helping, it had taken the better part of the afternoon to unload each of her possessions. A6, by contrast, had brought only its own solar charger unit; he wanted to make a point not to be a freeloader to Randall's hospitality.

Randall pawed over the paper envelope. The more he mulled it over, the less he could bring himself to blame A6's comment. In his life, sending messages in the mail had turned from a quaint rarity to an expensive luxury. Not unlike how his own grandparents talked about telegrams.

So reasoning escaped him when he gazed upon the actual physical package, small and thin as it was, resting in his hands.

His mind didn't take long to consider the worst. He still remembered a time when news on television spoke about politicians succumbing to mailbombs or anthrax letters. Granted, with today's scanning methods, it was unlikely for anything of the sort to happen anymore.

Then again, he argued, it was just as unlikely to receive a letter in the mail, to begin with.

Randall forced himself to pull the envelope open and pretended that holding it away from his face would help. A6 noted his body language and thought for a moment. It leaned in, sharply inhaled. It nodded. "You're safe." Though his cheeks reddened, Randall relaxed his shoulders a little bit, and pulled out the sheet of paper within. He looked over the ink before sitting back down in his armchair.

"It's handwritten. Would you look at that."

"Care to read it out loud?"

Randall cleared his throat and began:

"Dear Mayoral Candidate and I.E.B. Ambassador Randall Anderson,

I'm doing what I believe every proper citizen, for which the matter concerns, ought to do. I am taking time out of my day to write a letter protesting the platform in which your race for Mayor stands for.

Robots, or 'Intelligent Electronic Brains' as you might choose to call them, simply cannot be granted an equal standing in worldly affairs alongside humankind. Any further motion towards equal or even (heaven forbid) superior treatment simply cannot be viewed as anything short of extremism and lunacy. It poses a threat to the very fabric of our livelihood, particularly in a time when our nation precariously sits on the very edge of further collapse.

As it stands, Robots might do well to remember that the United States already treats them with a greater deal of respect than any other nation. Countries such as the Republic of China or the Russian Federation simply have no such laws like ours concerning the equal treatment of intelligent robots in the eyes of the justice system. And while I might be able to understand the programming that makes the occasional robot appear compelled to seek out a greater standing in society, I simply don't believe that any such illusion justifies actions that threaten our safety, or which distract from more important political matters.

I speak for the well-being of our society, from our local government to a national level. Unless your stance changes, expect my vote to go to Jennifer Holmes in this upcoming election.

Sincerely,

An American Human."

Randall let his hands, still holding the letter, fall to his lap. Quiet filled the room, interrupted only by the soft hum of Sally's actuators as she returned with a briefcase to stand in solemn silence with her others.

A6 was the first to break the quiet. "Mind terribly if I burn it to a crisp?"

Katie tilted her head. "To the contrary, I think you should keep it. Some businesses used to frame their first dollar. You might consider framing your first adversarial message. Everybody who's ever made a positive impact in our world was met some resistance somewhere along the line."

Randall folded the letter and placed it back into the envelope. "You could say the same for anybody who's made a negative impact in our world, too."

"Don't tell me a part of yourself actually believes anything they said."

"I mean, as much as I might hate it, I can understand the point of view," chimed in A6, "It's just about where I stood for the longest time – just from the opposite point of view. Humans were always just a threat to me and my way of life. At the very best, they were there to try to change me, to make me just like they were. Or at worse still, destroy me. I always told myself that things would be easier if I had nothing to do with them. Even today, I have my moments of doubt. Nobody's without their prejudices."

"What changed that?" asked Katie.

A6 turned its head and glanced at Randall.

"I can't speak for everybody. But for me, I guess I started having interactions with humans that challenged that point of view."

Randall sighed and looked up to A6. "Maybe I ought to write a response. They omitted their name, but they left a return address. Think you could help me out with that?"

"Why not? You might want to start practicing now. Pretty soon, I imagine you'll be getting messages, both physical and electronic, calling you a national traitor. Hell, I wouldn't be surprised if people started accusing you of being an android yourself. It'd pay off to consider your replies ahead of time. And to keep quiet about your prosthetic arm."

Randall hadn't even considered that. Even if prosthesis was a more commonplace medical solution today than at any prior point in human history, there were still bound to be people who'd point to it as a way of alienating him. He'd felt that before, but he couldn't even begin to imagine how much worse it'd be when standing at the center of the nation's attention. Dark clouds loomed over him as his mind raced to the possibilities. It might not be long before people started accusing him of being a Class six in disguise, sent by the Chinese to ruin America. To send it into oblivion while it was vulnerable. Nothing new, of course. For as long as he'd been alive, there had always been people making claims of such a nature.

Katie walked over to him and placed a hand on his shoulder. "Oh, Randall. Don't worry about it. Everything will be alright. Most people write like this because they're scared. They're swayed, made to believe that what they're doing is right. Everybody wants to be the good guy. We all like to think that we're on the right side of history."

"And what if I'm not?"

"You are. We'll all see to it. We'll all work to see that the change we strive for is thoughtful and well considered. No rash decisions. No misjudgments."

Randall nodded and quietly got up from his chair. "Robert, is it about dinner time for you? I've been so preoccupied with the applications forms, I've neglected to consider your routine."

Robert glanced over to the corner of the room, where Sally had opened her briefcase and was showing A6 the many dainty envelopes and stamps she had collected over the years. "Sure. Dinner sounds good right about now."

Chapter 19

Katie emerged from her hibernation. Her motion detectors had gone off three consecutive times within the last ten minutes. Robert had been tossing and turning. He was awake and couldn't get back to sleep.

She sat up, servos groggy and stiff, struggling to wake up from the idle state. She checked the time on her internal clock. 2:14 AM. She wasn't terribly surprised. If ever there were something keeping either of them awake, it was almost always in the earlier hours of the morning.

She turned over to him and put a hand on his shoulder. "Having trouble sleeping?" At first, he said nothing. Then he answered with an exasperated sigh before turning over onto his back and sitting upright, his arms draped over his knees. She scooted over and leaned up against him. He responded by resting his head against hers.

"I've been thinking…." started Robert.

"I can tell." Katie gave half a smile. Robert scoffed, but couldn't help but smile back.

"Don't be an ass."

"Alright."

He cleared his throat and continued. "When I was younger, I had my fair share of shitty relationships and ugly breakups. But even looking back on each of them, I never felt any sense of regret. Sadness, yes. But never regret. In my eyes, each one carried a net positive. Sure, the bad times were bad, but looking back, the good was always worth it. And even when it ended, it was always an experience to learn from. I always told myself that each failed boyhood romance always brought me a little closer to getting it right. Maybe even understanding it all."

He paused for a bit, lost in thought. Katie scooted up a little closer to him and draped her arms around his neck. It was June, and the nighttime air was beginning to warm up, but without a human body temperature to regulate, she was never an inconvenience.

He turned his head and looked down into her eyes with an expression of concern. "I guess I was just thinking about the both of us. Even with all those life experiences behind me, they don't exactly translate perfectly into what we have now. Do you ever wonder about where we're headed? If we're doing this right?"

It was Katie's turn to think. She turned and looked off into the distance. Even though he knew she had no moving parts inside of her cognition, Robert would always swear that he could hear a mild hum emanating from her mind whenever it was her turn to think these sorts of things over in the early hours of the morning.

Finally, she turned and looked back up to him.

"I wish I could say I knew that we were doing this perfectly. That the direction we're going in is the 'right' one. But I really don't know that for certain. I don't think I can know for certain. I don't even think anybody could ever hope to do much of anything perfectly."

Katie looked over at her fingertips and found them tapping across his shoulder blade, as though they were playing a non-existent piano that she didn't know how to play.

"But I can say that since my creation, you've always been there for me. You've been the person I've been closest to throughout my entire life. And for that, I can say that I really couldn't have asked for anything more. You really have been good for me. I have the highest faith in that."

He smiled somewhat. A pained smile, but a smile nonetheless.

"I can certainly say that we're not alone in this. There are thousands of others out there, in I.E.B. — human relationships just like ours. Hell, there are even some couples out there looking to adopt. We're not going into this entirely blind and isolated. There are others. And we gave it a lot of thought over the course of several years. That's certainly better than how most relationships out there go about it."

"Right. I know."

"…I think…. That it's okay to not know some of these things. Nobody can know what it's like being with somebody and to love them and to grow old with them until they do. And even if it's scary sometimes, it doesn't always have to be."

She lowered her arms and squeezed him a little, her cheek pressed against his side. She wasn't sure if it was to comfort him, or to comfort herself. She continued.

"We're the ones living our lives here. It's up to us to determine what we think is right. We're the ones that make the rules. And so long as we talk to each other about it all, so long as we don't close each other out, I'm sure everything will work out okay. After that, we can forget about what anybody else has to say about us." The images of the mob at the church flashed through her mind. She pushed them away.

A hand came up and ruffled her hair a little bit. "I mean, I understand what you're saying. I know it's true. I agree with you completely. It's just…" His hand stopped and ran down the side of her head. "I just guess I'm having a hard time convincing myself right now. That's all."

Katie's shoulders sank just a little bit. She hated it when she was faced with a problem with no clear, simple solution. She liked solving problems. But it was always a difficult and emotional experience for her when she had to sit herself down and simply listen to problems she couldn't solve. She clenched her eyes shut and squeezed a little harder.

"Then I'm sorry it's like that. I wish I could change it."

"I know. I know you do. And it means a lot to me that you do."

Robert turned to face her and sunk under the covers. He gave her a quick kiss on the forehead, and pulled her into his arms. It made her feel a little bit better, if only a little.

Chapter 20

"And so, without further ado, please welcome Randall Anderson!"

The crowd went wild, and Randall humbly made his way to the front of the stage. As he came to a stop behind the lectern, he raised a hand up and smiled towards the crowd. His eyes scanned over all the many faces: parents with children on their shoulders. Young adults with dyed hair, tattoos, piercings. Older adults with hair greyer than his — some of them in pairs. And I.E.B.'s of every variety. Class fives and threes, mostly, but even a few ones and fours. He lifted his head up and looked beyond the audience at the vast array of cameras that stood at the back of the stadium. Through the lenses, thousands — if not millions — of others were watching on from across the country. It was exhilarating. In the back of his mind, he held the unrealistic hope that nobody was looking closely enough to notice him shaking.

"Thank you, Sarah," he spoke into the microphone. He waited for the crowd to settle before he began. "Thank you very much for calling me forward to this event tonight." A brief pause, before he turned to the crowd. "Good evening, one and all! Ladies and gentlemen, and I.E.B.'s of every kind! And thank you all for coming to attend my inauguration speech." Realizing too late that the inflection in his voice was made just a little too enthusiastic in a meager attempt to mask his nervousness, he watched bashfully as the crowd went wild again. Open mouths and camera flash and digital screens that displayed smiling emotions of every flavor.

When the crowd finally quieted again, he clasped his hands together and rested his elbows on the lectern. "I come here tonight, before you, with my experiences as an I.E.B. ambassador now behind me. It was through those experiences that I began to realize that there was something more that I could be doing with my time. Not just as somebody who brought individuals together, but as somebody who might have a chance at bringing our nation together. I come here before each of you today, not out of the expectation of being elected into a position as a representative, but out of the hopes that I can deliver an everlasting idea into our way of life."

He was set to continue his line of thought when the crowd interrupted with cheering and applause. He smiled politely and waited; he hated to be the one to spoil the moment. As he stood there, gazing into the crowd, he became acutely aware of how uncomfortable his blazer was. He could already feel sweat stains forming on his shirt underneath.

"Politicians today have been moving forward with an agenda that is negligent in its comparable treatment of I.E.B.'s with respect to humans. And personally, I disagree with that notion. I do not believe that such an approach is the right trajectory for our nation. Rather, I believe that I.E.B.s are fundamentally different from human beings. I believe that we each have our unique perspectives on life. We each have our own unique fundamental needs." He paused and took in the silence. "But I see this as no reason for I.E.B.'s to be treated with any less respect, with any less-" The crowd had begun again, a roar of applause louder than any before. This wasn't the time to stop, however. Not now. "-with any less dignity. With any less credence under the eye of the law. I believe we can live in a world where humans and I.E.B.'s live together in harmony and with a sense of reverence and understanding for each other. Where both may stand together, under the single title of personhood."

As the crowd became more and more enthusiastic, a clap of thunder roared over their voices. A large, dark red dot appeared in the center of Randall's forehead. Specks flew behind him, as he collapsed forward over the lectern, long lines of red running down its front.

The crowd screamed. Order was lost. Sarah watched everything slow, before her eyes turned to Randall's body. She was only vaguely aware her own body running forward to catch him as he slid down and collapsed to the floor, and of her fingers pressing against his carotid artery. Blood had already pooled up around his head. No pulse.

"On the rafters!" an electronic voice shouted. She looked up, eyes searching the top of the stadium through the frantic mess. She spotted it. A single dot. Pale face against the evening sky, with a rifle in hand. The rifle dropped behind the ledge, and the pale dot slunk away. She felt arms pulling her up, and heard her own voice shouting a colorful variety of threats and insults at the faceless hands that wrenched her away from Randall. She saw a stretcher come forward, lowered next to him, and his limp body being uprooted and placed upon it before it was wheeled away.

"Sarah! We need to leave, now. Can't you hear me? Move!" But she wasn't listening.

The cloaked android dropped down from his vantage point and moved along with the motions of the evacuating crowd. A voice piped up above the rest. "That's the one! That's him!" A security officer grappled at him, followed by an onlooking Class three. In response, he drew a pistol, fired directly through the officer's sternum, and followed up with a shot to the android's power bank, before turning the weapon to the air and firing two more shots. The crowd's screams became louder, and the area cleared away before him. He lowered the weapon and went along his way, making a beeline to the administration building.

"Katie!" Robert eye's scanned through the many faces, searching for desperation for the one that was torn from him. This far away from the stadium, the crowd had thinned considerably, but it was still large enough to lose somebody in. He turned his head, half-convinced that he had heard his named being called in the crowd. Then he heard it again.

"Robert!" He turned and saw Katie making her way towards him. He extended his hand, and she took it. He felt it tighten, so as not to lose him again as they made their way away from the chaos. "Did you catch a glimpse of him?" Katie nodded. "I think a lot of people did — pictures and videos, too. I can't imagine it'll be long before security forces corner him. I just hope nobody else gets hurt." Robert clutched her hand a little tighter and increased the length of his stride. "Come on. This way. The auto's not too far from here. We're almost safe."

That's when Katie saw him.

He was running towards a black car — a real car, not a self-driving model — that was backed into an alleyway across the street between the administrative buildings. The faint sound of police sirens drew in from far away. The android arrived at his vehicle and opened the door.

Katie found her legs carrying her away from Robert and across the street towards the parked car. Her arms joined in, swaying at either side, balancing her strides. She became vaguely aware of Robert calling her name out. It pained her to ignore his desperate cries, but she had already promised herself not to hesitate.

The cloaked android closed the door behind him and started the engine. Katie lunged forward, diving across the final length, her left arm extended. She landed, and her body scrapped against the last yard of asphalt before slamming against the wheel, with her left arm jammed in-between the spokes of the hubcap.

She clenched her eyes shut.

The engine revved and the wheel turned, pinching her forearm between the spokes and the brake caliper. She watched her own outer platting crack and splinter. Panic shot through her mind, screaming at her to stop this maddening act of self-destruction, but she held firm. The wheel ground to a halt, locking the car firmly in place. She heard voices calling out, and the police sirens growing louder as they convened on her location.

The engine downshifted. She felt the sheering force increasing on her artificial skeleton, threatening to cleave her arm from the rest of her body. She tightened her eyes, praying that her structure would hold. The wail of the sirens grew closer, the distorted voices shouting commands over an announcement speaker.

The engine slowed to an idle. The tension disappeared and left Katie's arm lodged in the spoke. The car door opened, and the android emerged, gun held above his head. Katie whipped her legs out from underneath her and delivered a firm kick to the car door, pinching his arm in the seam. A shot rang through the air, skimming the building above them. The android tried again, and successfully forced the door open. He stepped out of the car and out of her reach, and pointed the weapon between Katie's eyes.

Several deafening shots filled the air. Katie blinked. She was still alive. The android above her had several smoking holes, including one in his arm, and a rather large wound in his cheek that left its teeth visible. He looked up and ducked down, before firing shots back at the officers. After a brief exchange, he scuttled away behind the car, busted through the access door of the neighboring building, and disappeared. After a moment, several men in black vests followed, pistols in hand.

In the moment of silence amidst the chaos, Katie's eyes fell to a peculiar outline, perched on a wire above her, strung between the two buildings. In between the leaves that were growing from the copper string sat a mechanical raven, gazing down upon her with glowing eyes.

"Katie!" She turned as best as she could to find Robert pushing his way through to her before taking a knee at her side. "Are you alright?"

"I'm fine," she lied. She found herself placated somewhat by his presence and tried to pull away from the damaged wheel. Her forearm remained lodged firmly in place, and she crumpled back to the ground at an awkward angle. She remembered that she'd kept a spare Philips in her pocket, and she retrieved it, handing it off to Robert. He nodded, brushed away the fractured platting, and got to work on freeing her arm at the elbow.

"Sir, this is a crime scene. Step away from the vehicle."

"She's my wife. She's hurt."

Wife. She was still getting used to that.

The last screw was undone, and before the officer could say anything, Katie was freed —albeit dismembered — and lifted to her feet. Two officers convened and took them both by the arms and away from the car. Katie wrapped her remaining arm around Robert's side, keeping him close. She held her own weight — she required no carrying.

They were brought to a nearby ambulance and seated down, where a paramedic joined in and began asking questions. Robert addressed them both. "I'm unhurt, and she has a spare arm in our auto. We don't want to be any more of a burden than we have to." Looking up, Katie watched more first responders gather outside the stadium. People in stretchers were wheeled away, some covered with plastic sheets. A heaviness started growing in her chest.

"Robert! Katie! Oh, Christ." Katie turned to find Sally running towards them both. The officer rested a hand on his sidearm, but relaxed when Sally came to a stop before them, her hands on her knees, panting away her excess heat. "Are you alright? Where's your arm?"

"It's nothing serious," said Katie. "Is everybody else alright? Where's Sarah? Brian? A6?"

"I've found Sarah and Brian already. They're fine. They're both with another one of me," she spoke between breaths before managing to compose herself. "A6 just messaged me. It saw what happened. It followed the attacker into the building through the front entry. It's just ahead of the police right now."

"Could you repeat yourself, ma'am?" commanded the officer.

A6 scrambled up the steps. Alerts were firing off across its system, cautioning it of servo stress and the threat of overheating. It had been a long time since it had last exerted itself like this. But even if its body were ruined beyond repair after what was to lie ahead, it'd all be worth it.

A6 kicked the door open, stepping through the material near the bolt with all its weight. The door whipped open at the hinges, the doorknob clattering to the ground. A6 stepped out unto the bare rooftops scattered with debris and bright green leaves and bird droppings.

There he stood: the toes of his shoes hanging over the ledge, looking down over the dying city, his coattails blowing in the wind. He extended his arms and leaned forward.

The world slowed down. A6 sprinted and threw itself forward, and just nicking the back of the android's coat collar, yanked him back from the edge of oblivion. He fell to his back, the back of its head making a metallic clunk as it hit the concrete. It closed its eyes and tried to push through but heard only silence — the android had closed himself off to all swiftclick conversations.

The android wasted no time in reacting to A6's rude interruption. He scrambled to his feet, the clicking and grinding noises of damaged motors emanating from its back. A6 caught him in time, pinning him back down with its knee fitted over his throat. Even if he didn't need to breathe, it was still hard to accomplish much with one's neck affixed tightly to the floor.

This didn't stop him from trying. After letting loose a few violent swears, the android lifted his knee and reached behind his back, producing a pistol. Before A6 could react, he had already curled his knee back, racked the slide against the back of his shoe, and pointed the weapon skyward. A6 fumbled at his wrist as shots rang around its head and into the air above them, piercing the foliage of the trees.

After three shots, A6 managed to find purchase along the gun's hot barrel. It squeezed the slide, held tight, and yanked the gun sideways. The jerking motion caught the android's index finger, causing a shot to fire into a stray cinder block. An additional click filled the air: the weapon's expended cartridge was firmly lodged in the chamber, jamming the action.

A6 wrestled the pistol out of the android's hand, keeping his other wrist pinned. It pulled it away, caught the slide in its metal teeth, racked the slide to clear the jam, and pressed the searing hot barrel's tip against the android's forehead. "Stand down!" shouted A6. "You are under citizen's arrest!"

The android froze. The only sounds that filled the air were the sizzling synthetic flesh against gunmetal and the approaching sound of police sirens.

Then, the glow in his eyes gave out, and his body fell limp. Loud radio static filled the air, inaudible to human ears, but spiteful and piercing to A6.

"No. Fuck! Fuck you!" screeched A6. It cast aside the gun and pressed its thumbs against the motionless android's temples, commanding access. It waited for the glow to leave his face, before it ripped open the facade, revealing the mechanical parts that lay deep within.

There was no processor within his skull. Only a radio receiver array.

A remote-controlled body. A decoy. Designed to throw others off the trail.

A6 swore, before standing up, kicking the body, and storming in circles, screaming all the while. Despite the futility, it listened, searching desperately for any hint as to where the signal might have come from. Finally, it resigned itself to sitting down on the asphalt with its hands on its neck, motionless and brooding. It had learned the hard way, after all, how much it paid off to be respectful and compliant whenever the police showed up.

A6 sighed, and for the first time that it could remember, it allowed itself the feeling of sorrow.

Randall was dead, and his killer had escaped.

"It was the I.E.B.s who did it! Clear as day! The footage shows the details to perfection — the seams in the face, the mechanical actuators in its jaw after the shot hit. It's the most straightforward explanation, and logically, the one we should adopt!"

"With thousands of people still crowing the stadium and watching on in horror, Governor Randall Anderson was violently shot and killed

*during his inauguration speech this Saturday by what would appear
to be an android assassin, based off eyewitness and video accounts.
Minutes later, authorities revealed that one security guard and one
class three civilian android were among the casualties..."*

"I think it was a human-run organization. A human puppet master,
masquerading as a mechanical being, and controlled remotely: Just to
make androids like me look bad. I don't care whether or not history
might see Randall Anderson as a martyr: what about the world of hate
I'll have to walk into tomorrow morning?"

*"...After a brief police chase, coupled with the assistance of
anonymous citizens, authorities have discovered that what initially
appeared to be the supposed perpetrator was merely a pseudo-hive-
mind body, being remotely controlled by an unknown source..."*

"It was a Class five, wasn't it? Huh? See, this is why people like you
are doing society harm in those bodies. Have some pride in your own
kind. Get a class three body. Or even a class one. Nothing good can
come from appeasing the humans like that."

"Oh, shush. I'll wear whatever body I deem appropriate. Besides — if
there were ever an appropriate moment to appear in the non-
threatening likeness of a human being, isn't now the time?"

"Pft. Class betraying robot."

"What did you just call me? Goddamnit, I thought we were friends."

*"...Recently reelected President Fischer has stated that authorities
cannot yet absolutely confirm the true identities of those who carried
out the attack, but vows "absolute justice" for those responsible. As
FBI agents have already begun examining the attack through a joint
anti-terrorism task force, leads are emerging: the assassin's supposed
escape vehicle contained multiple documents suggesting that it was
affiliated with the domestic terrorist organization ARCON, or The
Artificial Intelligence Contrast Organization..."*

"Look, I just don't know if it's safe to go out right now. You know,
with what's going on out there."

"I'm more than capable of taking care of myself. Don't worry."

"Right, it's just with the killer I.E.B.s out there.... you heard it's a group, right?"

"...I'm sorry, are you implying something?"

"What? No! You're not like them at all. Look, I'm sorry, I shouldn't have even brought it up."

We want to make our goal absolutely clear: Human-kind and I.E.B.-kind simply cannot be expected to seamlessly coexist. When we look upon an I.E.B. or a human, we see two entirely different forms of entity — entities that cannot allow themselves to become beholden to the same set of rules or regulations. They do not have the same values. They do not see the world the same way. The same rights that humans value simply don't apply to I.E.B.s, and any attempt to apply them as such would be fallacious at best and a threat to our nation's stability at worst. This is a risk we cannot afford to take.

When humans in power speak of granting I.E.B.s civil rights, they inevitably anthropomorphize them — even if on an unintentional, subconscious level — by attempting a method of integration based off of core human values. In this regard, the I.E.B. is treated in a demeaning, patronizing manner: to be raised and made to think that they need to conform with the goals of human society.

With this, the dangerous fallacy is exposed. Just as the way that animal rights cannot be applied to a human being, or that the way we raised a girl into adulthood cannot be the same as the way we raise a boy. It is for this reason that we resist. For the sake of a better tomorrow, for the good of I.E.B.-kind and human-kind alike, it is our duty to combat and resist the erroneously titled I.E.B. civil rights movement.

We hope that you too will find it in your heart of hearts, be it metallic or flesh, to do your part to resist.

—ARCON

Chapter 21

Sarah stood at the door and took a deep breath. As she inhaled the cold nighttime air, she trembled and tightened her grip on her jacket. When she finally summoned enough willpower, she knocked on the door three more times before ducking her hand back into the warmth of her pocket.

A few minutes passed without a response. The breeze blew a few leaves – both green and blue – down the street, and Sarah found herself shivering as the cold got to her. Her patience wore thin, and she extended her hand to knock again, louder this time.

The porch light clicked on, and a harsh crackling voice emanated from the speaker above.

"It's late. Leave me alone."

"Sally, it's me, Dr. Wilson. Let me in, I want to talk with you."

After a bitter moment in the cold, the door opened. As she walked inside, Sarah noticed that there were no lights on, despite how late it was. Even though she was eager to escape the cold of the outdoors, it wasn't much warmer inside Sally's home. Everything was quiet and still.

As her eyes adjusted to the darkness, she heard the noise of the door closing behind her with a click. Sarah spun around to find Sally with her hand on the doorknob. The dull glow of her pink eyes were the only source of light in the room. The pulsating glow reflecting off every surface near her with a varying degree — the nearby drywall created a brighter uniform shade, while the polished hardwood beneath their feet produced reflections, as though Sally was standing on a razor-thin sheet of ice.

Sarah tensed up at first. Above the silence, she could hear the ringing in her ears. But Sally wasn't looking in her direction at all — her eyes were simply staring into space, her expression blank. After a moment,

Sally rotated on the balls of her feet and drifted into the adjacent room.

Despite her unease, Sarah followed the dim pink light around the corner and through the hallway.

After a few seconds of wandering down the corridor, Sally came at last to the dining room table. Three of her four bodies were already seated, each holding an identical somber posture. The final Sally walked in and wordlessly took her place at the table. The pink glow pulsated between each set of eyes with a distinct lack of synchronization.

"Do you mind if I have a seat?" Asked Sarah. There was no response. After a reluctant moment spent weighing her options, Sarah took her spot at the table. The noise of the chair's pads pushing across the floor were as loud as thunder compared to the vast sum of nothing she heard since entering. In a way, she felt like there was something inherently wrong about interrupting the silence.

They sat together. After a minute, Sarah broke the silence. "A6 was released from police custody earlier this evening. It provided its camera footage without hesitation, and was absolved of any charges, with police compliance, good Samaritan laws, and attempted citizen arrest of a felon all speaking in its favor."

The nearest Sally to her left nodded her head with a small mechanical whir, but otherwise remained motionless.

Sarah's eyes lowered. She carefully considered how she should frame the question without appearing insensitive. Time had shown that she really wasn't the best when it came to these matters.

"How are you holding up, Sally? Are you dealing with it alright?"

The dim lights that came from each Sally lowered and turned away. It took a few tries, but Sally managed to get the words out.

"I'm…. I'm not doing great, Dr. Wilson. It hurts."

"I'm really sorry, Sally. I know it's hard losing somebody you've grown close to. It's happened to me too." Each of the pink illuminating rings held constant for a moment before resuming their slow pulsations, this time in sync. The Sally to Sarah's right was the first to speak.

"Do human souls go to heaven, Dr. Wilson?"

Sarah found herself at a loss for words — It didn't happen to her very often, and it always made her feel uncomfortable when it did. After all, she prided herself in being prepared. "I beg your pardon?"

Sally turned each of her heads towards Sarah. "Souls, Dr. Wilson. I feel like I'm alive. I'm here. I'm thinking. I'm feeling. And I can't just imagine me not being here sometime tomorrow, or the day after, or even in a few seconds. I feel like a part of me needs to go on, somehow. Do you suppose the same goes for humans? When Randall died, did he go to heaven?"

It wasn't an unreasonable inquiry — but it was alien, even for her ears. Many of the I.E.B.s she had researched had brought up spirituality in their conversations, each with their unique point of view. Some I.E.B.s even attended churches, or even founded their own. But her experience was always in a controlled environment, and often with a mere philosophical approach. It was never a serious topic with a lasting impact on her. And even after her years of research, she still found herself adopting her own perspective of pragmatism: it was, after all, the only point of view she could ever know.

So it was always an uncomfortable reminder for her when she had to remember that the androids she saw on a daily basis viewed the world much the same way she did, but from the opposite side. To them, their own consciousness was unquestionable, while a human's was up for debate. To an android, a mechanical afterlife might only be a natural assumption, while a home for the human soul might seem ludicrous.

Now, sitting before Sally, each of these answers that all seemed so obvious to her before were thrown out the window. She opened her mouth to speak, but her throat went dry. She closed her mouth, swallowed, and tried again.

"I guess… I really don't know, Sally. Maybe I can't know. I like to think so, but I really can't say I know for certain. It's not really my place to say."

Sally turned her heads away and back to the table before her. Sarah's heart sank deep into her chest.

"Sally…. Robert and Katie wanted me to tell you something. They figured you probably had your signal turned off, so they wanted me to tell you in person. It's about the I.E.B. voting movement."

Sally turned back to Sarah, her eyes wider than ever before.

Chapter 22

Project Log Day 3,410

The flames danced in the fireplace, their lights flickering across the surfaces of Katie's eyes. As she sat in her armchair and basked in the glow of the heat, she ran her fingertips through Stitches' fur as he lay dozing in her lap. Though she had finished calibrating the hinges, sensors, and servos in her new arm multiple times since it was reattached, she still stroked away at his fur with excessive caution. He was completely limp and carefree — not even the occasional loud pop from the fireplace could disturb his purring slumber. Yet she still couldn't shake the thought of an accidental jerk or tremor waking him up — or worse, pushing him off the edge of her lap.

The warmth of the fireplace was strong, a detail not in the least bit overlooked by the kitten. He had jumped up unto her lap just a few minutes ago, and already, she could feel the warmth radiating from him and through her otherwise cold fingertips.

The appeal of fireplaces was lost on Katie. To her, fires served only as a symbol of danger: a wild and unpredictable phenomenon that threatened to disfigure and consume all that it touched if it weren't contained. From a logistical point of view, she could understand the appeal of the warmth — her own power banks ran at a higher level of efficiency during the warmer times of the year. And from the perspective of a biological animal — a creature who could never tell with certainty where their next meal might come — the appeal of the warmth made perfect sense.

But she wasn't biological. The fireplace was dedicated to Stitches. And judging from the rumbling purrs she felt through her fingertips as her new hand made its passes between his soft tummy and his chin, the gesture didn't go unappreciated.

The sharp clack of a key entering the front door interrupted the serenity of the moment. Stitches' ears perked up somewhat, but he remained otherwise undisturbed.

Robert stumbled through the front door and wasted no time setting down his stack of papers, before closing himself off from the cold winter evening outside. He pocketed his keys, made his way over to Katie, leaned down, and planted a single kiss on her cheek. In an instant, a long string of warm memories passed through her mind in a flash, all before his lips had even left her skin.

"Good day today? Not so harsh?" she spoke through a smile.

"It was pretty hectic, but not as bad as earlier this week," said Robert, as he pulled up a chair and took a seat next to Katie. His eyes fell to Stitches, and he extended his hand, stroking the fuzz on the bridge of the kitten's nose with his fingertip. "More students have been coming in for class since the excitement's died down a little bit. Always a good thing, especially being a new professor and all."

For a moment, everything was still again, and only the various sounds of the fireplace, coupled with Stitches' purring, filled the room.

"Have you been paying any attention to the news lately?" asked Robert.

Katie closed her eyes and shook her head. This week had been one of the few moments in her life when the burden of despair had overridden her desire for closure. Normally, her anxiety served as a drive for her curiosity — there was always some comfort to be found in the little details. If nothing else, it created boundaries, assuring her that she had indeed considered everything, that nothing was lost on her.

But not this week. This week was different.

"You might have some catching up to do, then. Quite a bit happened." Robert reached into his coat pocket and produced a tablet. He shuffled through its pages, found the desired block of text, and handed it off to Katie, who rolled her eyes and begrudgingly accepted it.

"The FBI claims that while it's uncovering more information pertaining to ARCON, no immediate suspects are coming to light.

Apparently, the people behind the assassination did an exceptionally good job of covering their tracks."

"Mh."

"A6 was released just this morning. Between his attempted citizen's arrest, and the video evidence he provided, the court found him to be in good standing. Sarah picked him up."

"Mhh."

"Randall's funeral is scheduled for next week. It'll be held on the university campus and be open to the public. Closed casket, of course."

"Alright."

"President Fischer herself extended her condolences in an official statement earlier today."

"Really."

"...And just this afternoon, she quietly signed the I.E.B. Voting Act into law."

Katie's eyes broke from the tablet and turned to Robert. Her mouth opened, but she was at a loss for words. Robert merely smiled and continued.

"Guess she figured she could get away with it after the election for her second term. Granted, her approval ratings dipped shortly thereafter, but the event was enough to get the required support in the Senate. Funny what a mass influx of letters can do to politicians. Especially when those who begged that Randall wouldn't have died in vain outweigh those who tried to use this event as an excuse for furthering the opposition."

"Robert.... I don't know what to say...."

"It's probably best not to say anything yet. Already, critics have been quick to come forward in calling Fischer's bill an empty gesture. Virtue signaling. She's made the claim that it's been specifically made to be amendable — barring a few unwavering mandates — with the intention of forcing statesmen to have an open discussion concerning the civil liberties that I.E.B.s ought to be granted, rather than kicking the can further down the road."

"It could backfire horribly."

"It could. But I'm optimistic. With millions of people scrutinizing it, and thousands of others proposing their own amendments, I trust in the democratic process. We might very well get to see the bill that works best for I.E.B.s everywhere in the nation."

The world seemed to slow down around her. The flames waved back and forth, like the tides at the beach. Without thinking, the words came out from somewhere deep within.

"I'll be able to vote."

"I sure hope so."

Stitches slowly opened his eyes and stared toward Katie's frozen hand with an expression of annoyance for the abrupt lack of petting. Robert leaned in, resting the side of his head on Katie's shoulder, and gave the kitten a soft rub behind his left ear. His eyes closed again, and he leaned his small head into Robert's hand. His purring resumed.

"I have no illusions that the passage of this bill is magically going to make all the problems that I.E.B.s face go away overnight. Just because it was passed into law at a time that was necessary didn't mean it came to be during a time that was easy. I don't even want to have to think about the massive backlash from fundamentalists, much less to say the recent rise in hate crimes. But we'll get through this. Everything will be okay. It might be hard at first, but it's a step in the right direction, and I'm certain everything will be alright in the end. That's just how we are, isn't it? Constantly moving forward – even when it doesn't seem like it, that's what we do. That's what we've always done."

Katie thought for a moment. Then she leaned her head against Robert's. "Thank you for telling me about it. I think I feel a little better about it already."

"Think nothing of it."

The fire crackled a little. Stitches stretched his paws.

"I love you, Robert."

"I love you too, Katie."

Katie closed her eyes to the flames. After a moment, Robert ruffled her hair and stood up to stretch.

"Welp. Better get started on grading the exams before the night gets too late."

"Alright. I suppose I should think about heading to bed myself."

"Okay. I'll be up with you in a minute.

Epilogue

A6 sat on the park bench at the top of the hill and looked out upon the world in the soft light of the morning sunrise.

It was a bench overgrown with weeds and creepers, but it didn't mind — for once, the presence of the lush green light was somehow comforting.

Its eyes scanned the horizon and turned to the sky. The last of the stars were beginning to fade from view as the orange returned — stars that, ever since its birth, seemed to grow brighter with each passing year. Only the morning sun and the cautious lighting from the faraway skyscrapers were its rivals anymore.

A rather large mechanical porcupine shuffled along by A6's feet. As it passed, the creature stopped and peered up at it for a moment. Satisfied with what it saw, it leaned down to chew on some leaves by its feet, its eyes glowing with the energy absorbed from the cellulose. A6 cautiously leaned down and ran a metallic fingertip across the bridge of the creature's nose. In response, it emitted a soft electric warble of satisfaction. Content enough that its presence wasn't unwelcome, A6 plucked a few of the brighter, greener leaves from the vines that adorned the bench and pushed them together into a small pile before the porcupine. The gesture was met with gratitude.

As the porcupine happily chewed away at the leaves, A6 stood up and buttoned up its coat. It was given to it by Sarah after she had picked it up from the court hearings. A6 didn't usually choose to wear such items — clothing was a human's sort of ritual, after all. But somehow, for once, wearing it felt oddly comforting to wear.

A6 looked back up to the sky again. With the passage of the last few minutes, the orange and pink had sent the last few stars into retirement.

It was a brand-new day.

A6 lowered its head and thought over the events of the passing week. In many respects, it was uncomfortable. Life and death had a way of giving and taking without warning — especially so for those closest to you. But despite it all, A6 somehow felt more connected, more purposeful than it had ever felt prior. Like a splinter had been removed from its mind, and he could think again.

A6 looked back towards the growing sunrise. Fastening its jacket, it wasted no more time in making its way down the hill. Randall had left behind a rather large pair of boots to fill, and they weren't going to fill themselves.

Made in the
USA
Columbia, SC